WALKING THE DARKNESS DOWN

The Redemption of Howard Marsh 5

Bob McGough

Bearded Bard Inkworks
www.beardedbardinkworks.com

This arc of the Jubal County Saga could be called
Found Hope.
So each part is dedicated to a different group who helped
me find my Hope as an author.

For the folks I consider my mentors:
Rachel Brune
John G. Hartness
Ben Meeks
Bobby Nash
Whether it be from the words you have spoken to me,
or the actions I have learned from,
mimicry is flattery, right?

Contents

An Introduction to Howard Marsh   IX

Hot Times By The Shores   1

Time I Collect My Bones   3

Flat Earth Space Lasers   6

Could You Describe the Ruckus?   15

A Little Dust on the Bottle   23

What Does That Have to Do with the Price of Tea in China?   30

We're Gonna Need More Wine   36

You Fool, It's Only Moonlight   42

So, to Each Their Own   49

I've Been Wandering in the Dark About as Long as Sin   56

Well, Damn — 67

Straight Shooter — 70

A Sumbitchin' Cat Burglar — 80

A Thin Chew of Tobacco — 89

Some Things Can't Be Unseen — 96

A Sumbitchin' Cat Burglar, Redux — 100

Into the Belly of the Beast — 105

Magic Is Sexy — 112

Was This Whole Story Just an Excuse for a Terrible Pun? — 117

The Tale End of the Shaggy Dog — 124

Nose To The Grindstone — 131

Rainy Thursdays, Am I Right? — 133

Friendly Chats — 139

Fill Your Pockets with Lead and Silver — 143

Fond Memories I'll Keep of Happy Ways — 152

But They Left Me in a Forgotten Place — 155

With No Hands Around Bones — 160

Coyote Grins — 164

Ooo, Foxy Lady! — 168

Forgive Me, I'm In Morning — 174

And the Weekends Come and Go Like Tides 178

Moon Is on the March 183

Kill the Headlights and Put It in Neutral 188

It Can't Rain All the Time 197

And Everything That's Golden and Green . . . 202

. . . Goes to Hell 208

In the Sun He Hides Away 216

How Have I Been Chased So Long 223

The Death of Coyote Woman 230

Oh, They're Reckless, and Baby, So Weary 238

You're Dead and Out of This World 242

Fruitful Harvest in a Wicked Garden off a Forbidden Tree 252

Epilogue 255

The Back Matter! 259

Struggling with Drug Addiction? 265

An Introduction to Howard Marsh

Howard Marsh is a lot of things: a liar, a thief, a poor man's wizard. He's a shoddily tattooed skin stretched over a too skinny body that's barely held together by the same drugs that are tearing his life apart. A cynic, his words are often as poison as the substances he takes to pass his days, a suicide attempt years in the making.

He's the scion of a family with a history as rich as it is materially poor. He's the product of a miserable county with more dirt roads than paved, where poverty and loss is the order of the day. He's a man haunted by his past, and has yet to find any reason to try and piece himself back together.

You would be well advised to take what he says with a large grain of salt. He will cover the worst parts, glossing over the bits that show his darkest sides. The bits where the drugs that ravage him are in control. Where we find him is at the bottom, eking out a living as a water witch, a copper thief, a finder of lost things. Living in a storage shed and trying to maintain what's left of his frayed relationships with the few family members who will still talk to him.

But dear readers, he's a better man than he thinks. He doesn't see it; he's long forgotten the possibility even, and no one left in his life sees it either. But, if you can endure the miserable existence of watching someone make nothing but bad choices for a time, then you will perhaps be rewarded. Maybe you will see him slowly scrabble out of the muddy, trash filled ditch that is his life.

It won't be quick, and it won't be painless. The stories to come are often filled with sadness. The fairytale ending is not for stories such as these. There is a chance at happiness, but it is a long way away, and there are many obstacles both in him, and in his path.

This is not a plea for understanding, or forgiveness, or any sort of justification. It is just the way of things.

He is Howard Marsh, the Methgician.

And he doesn't give a damn what you think.

Hot Times By The Shores

*Being the Ninth Tale in the Redemption of
Howard Marsh*

TIME I COLLECT MY BONES

In retrospect, setting up my fossil table at a church yard sale was, admittedly, not my brightest idea. On the flip side, though, I hadn't had to worry about getting hot, what with all the shade the good people of Elk Grove were throwing my way. And the squabblin' that broke out, well, that wasn't my fault . . . I mean, not really.

Lemme wind things back a lil bit.

You see, for weeks now, the idea of selling fossils and arrowheads as a side hustle had been gnawing at me. Though, to be a side hustle, I suppose you'd have to have a main hustle first. I don't think doing drugs counts in that regard, but the fuck do *I* know about entrepreneurship? Maybe stealing copper counts.

Either way, I was thinking it was time I started earning at least a little money in a somewhat legal fashion. It would make Anna happy, and I could then turn around and use said money for illegal purposes. It was a win-win in my mind.

Being the lazy little shit that I am, though, the idea had floated around my head like a bloated horsefly, as a lot of my ideas do, with no real gumption to get off the ground. But then the heavens opened up, the stars aligned, all that jazz: I found a nice TV tray table out back of the Christian mission that someone had left to be donated. It was wooden, and pretty damn solid. Well, solid for a tray table, I guess. But since it would fold flat, I could fit it in my shed easily enough and just whip it out when I needed it. And damned if it wasn't the perfect size for me to set up a few rocks and teeth upon.

Then, wouldn't you know it, not a half hour later I saw a flier taped up on the glass beside the door into the Piggly Wiggly for a community yard sale at the Lutheran Church starting up in a week. Every Saturday for a month they'd be holding these sales, with only a five-dollar fee to set up. The church was only about a half-mile walk from my shed, so I figured I could pretty easily carry what all I had over there—no car needed.

Even then, it probably still wouldn't have happened if I hadn't then found a five-dollar bill on the ground on my walk home. Now I know I can be a contrary cuss most times, but even I gotta bend to fate on occasion. So, I put that five in my wallet, and I vowed not to spend it over the next three days so I could use it for the yard sale.

. . . Well, that lasted about ten minutes, because it was hot as hell and I was carrying an armload of goodies, including my new table, and damned if the Dairy Queen wasn't between me and my shed. So, I used the bulk of that five on a dip cone and some fries.

Fate is one thing, but have you had a dip cone?

But anyway, I felt guilty after, so I ended up trying to borrow five bucks from Anna with a promise to pay her back when I sold some stuff. And because she's awesome and I don't deserve her, she agreed. And because she's smart, she said she would just pay the folks herself. Because, and I quote, "This, I gotta see."

There certainly was a show, so . . . she wasn't wrong.

Flat Earth Space Lasers

There aren't a whole lot of social events in Jubal County. I'm sure you are absolutely gobsmacked by that fact, but it's true. I mean, there would be rodeos on occasion down in Sumpville, and of course there was football in the fall. But most any other type of community gathering tended to be based out of a church. And since church folks and my folks tended to get on like two rats in a sack of grits, I never really found my way out into "polite society" much, you could say. Again, shocking.

After seeing the crowd that morning at Salvation's Cross Lutheran Church, though, I knew it wasn't a great loss on my part.

I was set up on the very tail end of everything, seeing as we were the last folks to show up. That meant that not so many folks made it down to our end of the rows of clutter-covered tables, but it did make for some of the best people watching. Which, hungover as I was, was about all I had in me to muster up.

Two rows of about twenty "booths" each were sat in a rough line running down the length of the back of the church. There was the brick church to one side, rows of sellers, then a couple of trailers that I guess were used for Sunday school for the kids or some such. Being last in the lineup, we had to make the walk of shame, carrying a couple of chairs, my table, and goodies right past every other family till we got to the very end, right up near the fence line that separated the church grounds from the surrounding neighborhood.

What you need to know about the Lutheran church is that it was the biggest church in town that catered to less snooty folks. The First Baptist had all the old-money folks—the mayor, the sheriff, all those kinda folks. It woulda never have done something so crass as having a *community yard sale*. So, while this was a church crowd that was set up, it wasn't like a CHURCH church crowd, if that makes sense—which I always thought was sorta strange, seeing as Lutherans had a lot more fancy of a sermon. Damn near Catholic, if you ask me, compared to the happenings at the First Baptist.

Anyway, because it was the Lutheran church, I think the community as a whole felt a little more welcome, and a little more loosey-goosey when it came to what was appropriate attire. In short, folks were treating this like a yard sale, not a *church* yard sale, or at least what I had imagined a church yard sale to be like. And that made for far, far better people watching.

Hell, I had worn sleeves, not wanting to be underdressed, and I was quickly learning that that had not been at all necessary. I considered pulling out my pocket knife and doing some impromptu surgery on my shirt before Anna had cut me the side-eye. And besides, it was one of my better shirts, a delightful little Down shirt I had stolen from a clothesline a few months back. So, the sleeves remained—for the moment.

The white trash pageantry was out in full force, however. For the men, it was usually some sort of variation of jeans paired with either a shirt (sleeves optional) with a flag (rebel or American) or something sports related (NASCAR or football). Unless the man in question was over the age of fifty, that is, in which case gray sweatpants were equally likely, and the shirt would shift to something very pro-Trump. Accessories ranged from openly carried pistols on the hip to oxygen tanks pulled along on little wheels. One geezer had the full set: a POW/MIA hat paired with a shirt bearing Trump holding both American and rebel flags, sporting his finery while struggling with one hand fighting to keep his sweatpants up under the weight of a too-large pistol clipped to his waistband and the other dragging his oxygen tank behind him. It was goddamn magnificent.

The ladies of the crowd had a lot more variety to them. They ranged from muumuu-wearing, rascal-riding meemaws to women who looked like they might be racing to see who could skirt the "ass hanging out the bottom of them Daisy Dukes" line the closest. A few especially harried-looking ladies, usually with a disturbing number of crotch gremlins hanging onto them while their husbands raised not one finger to help, had clearly just thrown on whatever was closest that morning. There were some bewildering displays of redneck peacockery to be seen, for sure. My favorite was the woman who had paired some camo-print crocs, cutoff purple sweatshorts, and a leopard-print top so low cut that she had to constantly battle the kid in her arms from tugging free one of her lady bits.

The less said about the kids, the better. I swear, they only knew how to speak in shrieks, and with my head splitting with a headache, I was really beginning to regret how much I had drank last night. Judging from the occasional groan emanating from my thickly sunglassed girlfriend beside me, she was feeling the same way. And kids being kids, every damn thing they saw, they wanted. Seeing as the parents were there no doubt to get a deal, they clearly weren't looking to spend a bunch on toys and shit, which naturally led to tears, and even more shrieking.

Luckily, more than a few parents just gave up and—I guess feeling at least *some* sense of embarrassment—either took their hellions home or bought them something to shut them up. So, by the time they made it over near where I had set up, well . . . they were almost tolerable. Not quite there, but enough that I didn't feel compelled to throw my sixty-five-million-year-old sea shells at them.

I had found about a dozen arrowheads in my wanderings in the past couple years, and those got snapped up within about thirty minutes of me being there. For a group of folks that probably spent a lot of time listening to Fox News bemoan the horrors that brown people were inflicting on this country, they sure were interested in anything to do with arrowheads. It was shitty, but then shitty folks' money needs spending, too.

I'd thought about trying to sell them for five bucks each, but that idea was pretty quickly shot to shit. These folks wouldn't have paid five bucks for anything short of a gold bar signed by Bear Bryant himself. In the end, I settled on a price of two dollars and got a perverse amount of joy in telling folks that I didn't haggle. Their gawping fish faces, mouths working open and shut like an angry bass, just gave me life in a way the shitty cup of coffee we'd gotten at the Dairy Queen couldn't.

Also, I didn't have or make change. Which wasn't a huge deal, seeing as by the time they got to me, every possible larger bill had pretty much been whittled down to ones. But one angry guy ended up having to pay five bucks for two arrowheads, and when I wouldn't budge to let him get a third, I thought his head was going to explode. Anna even managed to muster up a chuckle at that, which made him even more mad. It was glorious.

At one point, a long-haired fella spent an inordinate amount of time staring at my shirt. He even asked me if I was a Down fan, which, as I was, wasn't a hard question to answer. It made me wonder if maybe it had been his shirt I stole, but he didn't come right out and accuse me. He also didn't buy anything, which could have meant anything, or nothing.

The real highlight, though, was when someone asked about my fossils.

I had a box of shells, about nine or ten good-sized intact fossils. I mean, they mostly looked like rocks, but after I had washed them up in my Horace washing bucket, you could see the ridges on them. Sure, it might take a second, but more than a glance would tell you they weren't "just rocks." Besides that, I also had scraped up about thirty good shark teeth that I didn't mind parting with.

It was the kids that would, without fail, get the ball started, usually with some variation of "What's that?" followed by a grubby, sticky paw reaching out to touch my stuff.

"Don't touch!" I'd respond just before opening a can of worms. "Those are fossils. Most of them are over sixty-five million years old."

And then some form of argument would ensue with the parents. You see, evolution is real, the world is billions of years old, and it's also round as hell. But in Jubal County? Well, "We didn't come from no monkeys," "The preacher man says that God made the world six thousand years ago," and "Something, something, flat earth space laser, something."

Are there smart people in the County? Of course! Lots of them. Some of them even believe in facts and science and shit. Hell, most can even read. But this crowd? In this church yard sale? No, sir. The only facts here come up out the Bible, and I was a goddamn sinner, spouting such lies. And to children, no less!

Some of them kids didn't pay what I said no nevermind. Others agreed right along with their folks, joining in like properly little brainwashed minions, which was about what I expected.

There was one kid, though—a boy of about ten, I reckon—who had wandered up ahead of his momma while she was taking a good hard look at some books two booths away. He looked fractionally less sticky than most of the kids. A pudgy little bastard, he had on glasses beneath his strawberry-blond hair. Wonder of wonders, he didn't ask me what I was selling. Instead, he said, "Cool fossils," his eyes a little wide.

"Yep. Dug 'em up myself."

He was leaning in super close to look at the teeth. "Cool," he whispered, clearly entranced. I didn't respond, and he seemed content to just look on in silence. He gazed at each tooth in turn, then his eyes drifted to the box of shells. The arrowheads were all gone by that point, so I took some of the shells out of their box and set them out in the spot they had occupied so he could get a better look.

In a way, he kinda reminded me of a young me. Those few times I'd gotten to be around anything old, like fossils, coins, or arrowheads, I'd been happy as a pig in shit. Not that I ever got to buy any; we were way too poor for that. Probably why I had become a bit of a packrat these days.

After about a minute, he looked up from the fossils. His mom was calling his name, her romance perusing having profited her a small sack full of books, from the looks of things. He started to walk away, but I wasn't having that. I don't know what in the hell possessed me.

"Hey, kid," I said, causing him to stop. "You can have one, if you want."

You'd have thought it was fucking Christmas morning the way his face lit up. He stepped back over and, without a second thought, scooped up the closest of the shells. I had to admit, he had good taste—that was the one I'd have chosen, too, prolly. It wasn't the biggest, but it had a nice sheen on it and was the most clearly defined.

Did I get a "thank you"? Hell no. But I reckoned the look on his face was thanks enough.

"Gross," Anna said from beside me as the kid ran off.

"Yeah, kids suck," I said, though I was a little hurt, to be honest. Ya do something nice . . .

She raised up her sunglasses and leaned over. Blonde hair framing her face, she gave me a kiss on the cheek, right on the stubble. Then she leaned back into her chair and said, "No, kids are great. I meant it's gross how much I love you, Howard Marsh."

Well, that was alright, I reckon.

Could You Describe the Ruckus?

T hings started going sideways pretty quick. Because of religion, of course.

I wasn't paying too close attention to what all was going on behind the scenes as it were. I mean, if I had been, I probably wouldn't have been blindsided like I was. Not that the end result would have likely been different, but a boy can dream, you know?

The long and short of it was I guess someone got real offended that I was spouting "devil talk" in the corner of the church yard by talking about, ya know, facts. And being mature adults, they went crying to mommy, which, in this case, was someone who was some sort of deacon? He wasn't the preacher—I knew that, thanks to a bizarre series of events where I once got drunk with Pastor Kirkland.

This portly chap was no Pastor Kirkland.

He stood out in the crowd, as he was the only guy that was actually dressed churchlike. He had on a blue long-sleeve button-up shirt that had huge sweat patches on the armpits. He was bald as a jaybird, and since he had no hair, he had to keep wiping at the sweat on his brow with a handkerchief that he kept in his back pocket. It was soaked through, looking more like the remains of a drowned rat than a bit of fabric.

Even still, I wasn't paying him no nevermind, because I was marveling at the most magnificent mullet I'd ever seen. I swear that mullet had a man attached to it, not the reverse. If the damn thing had been a politician, I'd have registered to vote just so I could get it elected. It looked like a soft breeze was just constantly blowing through, the tips lifted on the wings of angels, no doubt.

So it wasn't until Anna gave me a nudge and said, "Here comes trouble," that I was able to tear my eyes off the second coming of our Lord and Savior Mullet Christ, but not before I vowed to myself that before the year was out, that I would be rocking a mullet of my own. 'Cause hell yeah.

Anyway, I shifted my gaze slightly and spotted Tubs parting the crowd like an icebreaker ship though the arctic.

It had less to do with his bulk, and more to do with the fact I think folks were afraid they would rub up against his sweat. Hell, get too close and you'd probably slip right off him and go flying.

The boy was *damp*, is what I'm trying to say.

But he was powering on toward us, heading straight for my little table without so much as a glance to either side. And fuck me if he didn't have a face like a wheezing red thundercloud. Happiness was far from on his mind, if I had had to guess, so I sorta sat up a little straighter and readied myself for some bullshit.

Did he introduce himself? Hell no, I was a sinner; I didn't rate that. He didn't even offer me a sweaty hand for me to refuse to shake because I didn't want pruney fingers. Nope, he just launched right into getting me riled.

"Son, you are going to have to go. Take your things and get on out of here, and don't bother coming back next month." He was keeping his voice low so that only Anna and I could hear it. The venom of it all was lessened by him dragging out the poor overworked rag to swipe angrily at the salty water threatening to drip into his eyes.

"You gonna give me a reason why?" I wasn't of a mind to really push things—not with Anna there, at least—but that didn't mean I was just gonna take it. I was pissed, but I wasn't about to cause a big ruckus at a church. Hell,

I knew the cops wouldn't even stop to ask questions; they would just see it was me and put me in cuffs.

"You can't come up here and try to corrupt our children and expect nothing to happen. So go on, git!" he spat.

"That's bullshit, but whatever. Give us back our five dollars, then," Anna said. I don't think I'd ever loved her more. She hadn't hardly moved an inch; she just sat there, all six and a half feet of her leaned back in her chair, looking as cool as a cucumber with her hand outstretched.

His eyes bulged at that. "Excuse me?"

I nodded. "You heard her. Give back the five we paid to set up here, and we'll go."

"That ain't happening! That's the church's money—you shoulda thought about that before you started spoutin' off nonsense!" He was steadily getting louder, and I don't think he realized it. But I could see behind him, and folks' eyes were starting to drift our way.

Anna frowned and got to her feet. She was a good eight inches taller than Ol' Boy and, I had to admit, was lookin' fine as hell. She had legs for days, and the jean shorts she was wearing showed off about every inch of them . . . which probably wasn't doing her no favors with Captain Preachy. I know the Lamb of God band shirt she had on definitely wasn't going to, once he noticed what she had on. "We paid to be here till two, and it's not even noon yet. Either give us the money, or go on and leave us alone."

He stepped closer then, clearly about to get all up in her face, but his gut bumped my table, causing it to rock back. As luck would have it, most of my stuff was up against the back side, so when it tipped a little, the weight of my wares did the rest, causing it to fall back onto my lap. I took a box of fossils to the crotch, which fucking hurt.

I sorta lost track of things there for a second as my future kids' lives flashed before my eyes. But by the time I got myself sorted, he and Anna were going at it in one hell of a shouting match. With the table out the way, they were able to get *all* up in each other's faces, Anna looking down and him looking up, the language growing steadily more colorful and creative. Tubs was gonna have to do a lot of repenting for more than a few of those words.

I thought about throwing in my two cents, but I was smart enough to know that with a reputation like mine, ain't nobody had time for what I had to say. Besides, Anna had it covered. So instead, I just sorta started tidying things up, getting ready to run. I knew it was just a matter of time before one of them did something irreparably stupid, and I just mouthed a quiet prayer that it wasn't gonna land me in jail. Again.

I was bent over picking up a couple of my spilled fossils when Ol' Boy, generations of "we don't hit women" no doubt drilled into his brain, totally lost his cool. And since he couldn't hit Anna, he lashed out by kicking my table. Which, with me being bent over like I was, meant it went colliding with my temple.

Least that's what I learned after the fact, seeing as it took me right out the game for a good five seconds as I sprawled back on the grass tangled up in my lawn chair, wondering what the hell happened. I think I heard an "Oh shit!" from a male voice. I know I heard Anna shouting "What the fuck?!" I didn't really care about the conversations, because I was just trying to remain conscious, a battle I was mostly winning—unfortunately.

There was a brief moment where I had an absolute crisis of faith of sorts. Like…why me? What was it about my life that meant I couldn't even sell rocks at a yard sale without a fight breaking out? Anna had the core of it: what the fuck?

Somehow the chair had folded itself up on my ankle, so as I tried to get to my feet, I just sort of fell back over. Anna was trying to help, but frankly I was in a bit of a daze, and I felt like we were working cross purposes. I fell at least two more times before we finally got my leg out of the chair. I'd given up on trying to stand at that point, just plopping my ass on the ground. Anna was crouched down, looking at my head, which, I gathered from her worried muttering, was showing a knot already but wasn't bleeding. Putting her nurse schooling to work, I reckoned.

Some church lady had stalked up and was dressing down my assailant. She was really tearing into him, which made me feel a little bit better. I thought for a moment that if I had done that, someone would have called the cops on me, no doubt, and I would probably be spending the night in jail. So, was it totally fair? Nah, but the embarrassment on his face was giving me life.

"Is he ok?" the church lady asked. She was about as short as me, but a good bit thicker and a whole lot older. Real grandmotherly type, dressed in a nice floral-print dress. All she was missing was a fancy hat to complete the look. I wanted to ask her where her hat was, but that may have just been the concussion.

"He may have a concussion," Anna replied. "Thanks to *that* asshole."

Grandma clearly had a bit of steel to her spine, and she put on a mighty powerful frown. "To be fair, you two should have just left when you were asked," she said in a firm tone.

Anna, I guess assured I wasn't going to die in the short term, rose back up and turned to face the woman. Crossing her arms, she said in an equally firm tone, "We would have, if he'd just given us back our money."

Church Lady glanced back at the man who had assaulted me, annoyance abounding on her face. Clearly, she had not been clued into the nuances of our debate. "Well that can be arranged. Brother James, pay her, and then let's help the Marsh boy inside out of the sun and take a proper look at him."

"I can walk myself," I said, getting slowly to my feet. I may have wobbled a little bit, but let's be honest, I'd handled a lot worse. Anna only had to help me a little, but she was brusquely moved to the side by the older lady.

"James, help her gather up their stuff, then come along to the kitchen. We're going to put a little ice on this lump," she said, taking me by the elbow. I thought about resisting, but damn if she didn't have fingers that grabbed my arm like bony little vise grips. So I just let her drag me along, and I did something I hadn't thought I would ever do again.

I set foot in a church.

A Little Dust on the Bottle

I didn't burst into flames, which was a pleasant enough surprise. And damned if it didn't feel pretty nice in there, what with all the air conditioning. I mean, lots of places have air conditioning, don't get me wrong, but I'd spent at least the last twenty-odd hours either in my shed or outdoors, so yeah, it was nice.

It was an old building, but they'd sunk a good chunk of change into it over the years, enough so that you couldn't really tell its age from the inside. There was some nice carpet on the floor, and the walls looked like they had seen a new coat of paint sometime in the past couple of years. I mean, it was all pretty bland and samey except for the occasional framed Jesus painting here and there, but that's about what you'd expect for a house of the lord, I reckon.

The old lady, who I'd since learned was Gretta Fitzpatrick, took me through a side door that opened up into a fairly long hallway. There weren't any lights on, but she flicked a switch I hadn't even noticed, and a second later the hallway went from "serial killer chic" to "normal church." The transformation hurt my eyes and head a bit, not gonna lie. Thankfully, we didn't have to go past too many doors for me to find myself in the kitchen.

Gretta got me seated at a small table in one of those hard plastic chairs like you would find at a school, then she set about trying to rustle up an ice pack for me. For some reason that seemed to involve opening every damn drawer and cabinet in the kitchen, then slamming them closed. Least that's how it felt to my aching head, and the bright white lights of the kitchen weren't helping much, either.

One of those cabinets was chock full of bottles of wine, though, that I did notice. If she'd have just offered me a couple of those I'd have called it even, then gone and drank until my head stopped hurting. But she didn't, instead rummaging with a purpose until she finally found the plastic baggies and a towel.

About the time she got the bag filled with ice and then wrapped up tight in a towel, Anna and James came into the kitchen. The A/C was cold, but the air between those two was positively frosty. If looks could kill, Anna would have already burned the whole building down with laser eyes.

Gretta handed me the ice pack, then turned to her minion. "I can handle it from here, James. Go keep an eye on things, if you would, please." She looked over to Anna. "You got your money?"

"Finally."

Her lips pursed, but Gretta didn't rise to the bait. "And you have your things?"

"I do," my girlfriend replied. Anna's arms were full of most of the stuff, and James leaned my little table up against the wall by the door. From the looks of it, that was everything, which meant I could now rest my eyes a bit against the glare of the lights.

"Rest here for a bit, then, if you please. I have to make a phone call, but then I'll pull my car around and drive you both home. Fair enough?"

I cut in before Anna could answer. Not bothering to open my eyes, I said, "Sounds divine. Thanks, Gretta."

The ice actually did feel pretty good—that, I had to admit. I reckoned I had taken a harder knock than I thought, because under normal circumstances, I'd have been raising holy hell. Gretta damn sure wouldn't be offering a *ride home*.

But I had my eyes on a bigger prize.

Opening my eyes a bit, I could see that Gretta was gone. With my free hand, I raised one finger to my lips so that Anna could see. She was about to set the box of our stuff on the counter, from the looks of things, which was perfect.

Getting to my feet, I hobbled over to the cabinets. My ankle was hurting me a little more than it had been, so I guess I must have twinged it a little when it got caught up in the chair. That was a problem for later Marsh, though.

Setting the ice pack down, I opened the cabinet where I had seen the wine. Sure enough, there were about a dozen bottles in there, each bearing the label of Mogen David. It was sacramental wine, but sacrament or not, it had an alcohol content. That was the best thing the Lutherans had going for them, I reckoned—all the other denominations in Elk Grove used grape juice, as if Jesus himself hadn't turned water into wine. Don't reckon they had Welches in ancient Israel, but then reasoning with Baptists on matters of faith was like arguing with me about, well, anything: just a recipe for a headache.

"What are you doing?" Anna hissed.

"Making amends," I whispered back. I grabbed up two of the bottles of wine from the shelf and placed them in the box of our stuff. The box was in no way deep enough to hide the full bottles, especially with what were left of the fossils. The necks of both bottles jutted out like flagpoles.

"What the hell?" she sputtered. "How is stealing their wine making amends with them?"

I paused, looking at her. I reckon I must have had one almighty confused look on my face. "It's not making amends with them; it's making amends with us. Emotional damages and all that. Plus, my head."

She looked at me for a moment, just sorta staring and blinking, like her brain was rebooting. Then she rolled her eyes and started opening drawers. "We need a towel or something to cover these up with."

I loved her so much. "My girl!"

I was only able to get one more bottle in; the box wasn't that big, after all. Still, three bottles would do us alright, I reckoned. Mogen David was who made Mad Dog 20/20, which had gotten me drunk many a time. But this stuff was a step up from that, and by a good bit. It wouldn't do for the good folks of Salvation's Cross Lutheran Church to have a sip of the Lord and have it be Mad Dog, so someone had opted for something a little higher up on the shelf.

I saw a roll of paper towels and took a few to wedge down between the bottles so they wouldn't clink together as we walked. See, that's the benefit of being with someone like me: the learned experience of shady shit. I'd once gotten chased out of, then banned from, a Citgo because someone had heard the two longnecks I'd managed to get in the back pocket of my JNCOs clinking together.

Lesson learned, and remembered. Squeezing in a bag of Cheetos between them would have saved me a whole world of grief. I wasn't gonna go down like that again.

About the time I got done tucking paper towels in most places I could easily reach, Anna had rustled up a bit of purple cloth. I was about 90 percent certain that it was the sort of purple cloth folks put on the crosses in their yards around Easter. Which struck me as perhaps just a touch too sacrilegious, even for me, but when you are stealing sacramental wine, I guess the bar is about as low as it can get. It covered things up well enough, and as long as we didn't let anyone get too close, I reckoned we would be alright.

"Aight, let's get," I said, grabbing up my table in one hand.

"Grab the ice pack," Anna urged as she slung one of the chair bags over her shoulder.

My confusion was back. "We can drink it warm . . ."

"For your head, jackass."

That made sense. So, I obliged. We each had one of the chairs, I had the table and ice pack, and she had the box and wine. We were all set.

I looked out in the hallway. The coast was clear. "Let's ride on outa here before Gretta comes back."

And that's just what we did.

What Does That Have to Do with the Price of Tea in China?

Well, I tell you all about our yard sale antics to explain why Anna and I were wine drunk at one on a Saturday. Because otherwise, things would probably have played out a good bit different. Not better or worse, most likely, just . . . different.

We made it back to the shed easily enough, without running into either Gretta or James. Maybe Jesus approved after all. That walking worked up a powerful thirst in the two of us, and wouldn't you know it, we had three bottles of victory wine, perfect for celebrating our successful morning.

'Cause it had been a successful, if messy, morning. Anna wasn't out any money, I had legally earned a decent chunk of change, and I probably wasn't actually concussed! Will wonders never cease?

Once back at the shed, we cracked open a bottle of wine and started pouring ourselves tall pours in this pair of old coffee mugs I had. They were bizarre, a somewhat matching pair that I guess had come from either Alaska or Canada, reason being that if you looked closely, you could see imprints of images of folks hunting seals. I'd seen them in the Christian mission—and actually *paid* for them, I was so entranced by how fucking bizarre they were.

The wine was warm, but it actually didn't taste all that bad. Certainly better than Boone's Farm and Thunderbird, though I realize that's a real low bar. I know some folks like to pair red wines with some types of food, and whites with others, but all that is beyond me. All I know is that the red we were drinking paired real well with the joint we passed back and forth.

We had just cracked open the last bottle when I heard the sound of tires on gravel that told me someone was coming into the U-Store-It. We'd finished the joint by that point, and since day drinking in a storage shed ain't illegal, we didn't make any move to stop. I was kicked back in my recliner while Anna had her length laid out across the couch, the wine sitting on a milk crate between us. Living the high life, just basking in the breeze of the oscillating fan.

So it was that we were both in a real chill sort of mood, all giggly, drunk, and stoned. Which is why neither of us kicked up a fuss when my ex, Lidda, came pulling up in a shitty little Ford Taurus that had clearly seen better days.

I hadn't really seen Lidda since I had started dating Anna. We used to have a habit of shacking up on occasion, even though we hadn't dated since high school. Some habits are just hard to break, I reckon, but I'd avoided the temptation so far and hadn't visited her in months. And since she never was one to visit me, this was admittedly a little odd.

She gave a little wave when she got out the car but didn't come over at first. Instead, she opened the back, where I could see a toddler in a car seat. She set about freeing the child, bent over more than seemed entirely necessary. Almost as though she was trying to stick her butt out and get the athletic shorts she was wearing to ride up past what was probably considered decent.

"That who I think it is?" Anna asked.

"Yep. Lidda."

Anna snorted and started to sit up. She knew about our history, but they'd never met, so far as I knew. Anna usually wasn't the super jealous type, but she also wasn't an idiot. "Those pants short enough, you think?"

I knew a trap when I heard it, so I just kept my mouth shut and decided to make sure that I was seen looking anywhere that wasn't the backside of my ex. "Wonder what she wants?" I asked, taking the opportunity to top off my not-very-empty mug. Anything to keep my eyes in safe places.

"Mmm" was all Anna had to say. I mean, that was all she said out *loud*. There was a whole-ass novel said silently, I felt. One I was in no hurry to crack open and read.

Soon enough, Lidda had pried the kid from its seat, and holding him on her hip, she came on over. She had a smile plastered on her face, but it didn't read as legit. It was forced, and there was some real worry there. Which would track—why else would she come calling unless she needed help?

"Heya, Marsh," she said as she stepped into the shadow of the shed.

"Lidda." I nodded, gesturing toward Anna with my mug. "This here's Anna, my girlfriend."

"Pleasure," Lidda said, forcing a smile in Anna's direction.

"I've heard so much about you, I feel like I already know you," Anna said.

"Oh, if I know Marsh here, you've probably only heard half the story."

If I hadn't been drunk and stoned, I'd have been freaking out, not gonna lie. They were like a couple of tomcats circling each other. So, I decided to just cut to the chase and see if we couldn't get the ball rolling here.

"So, what brings you by?"

Lidda frowned a little. "Can we talk in private a quick second?"

I knew how that would go over, so I nixed that idea straight away. "Anna's cool. Go ahead and say it."

"It's about . . ." Lidda made a sort of wiggly motion with the fingers of her free hand. She coupled it with a knowing glance.

She was the only one knowing, though; I didn't have a clue what the fuck she was on about. So, I asked real polite-like, "What the fuck are you on about?"

Frustration flashed on her face. "You know . . ." Again with that same stupid hand motion.

"What the hell—"

"Magic. She's talking about magic," Anna interrupted, impatient.

"Oh," I said at the same moment Lidda muttered an almost shameful, "Yeah, that . . ."

Lidda nodded toward Anna. "I didn't know if she . . . you know . . ."

"He tells me everything. Don't you worry about that."

I hadn't really ever had someone be, like, actually jealous over me before, least not in recent memory. It was kinda hot. There was a brief moment where I imagined the two of them going at it in a tub of Jell-O, but I managed to rein it in before my pants got tight.

"Yeah, she knows about me and all that shit. So, come on, out with it."

"Well, you see . . . I think my neighbors are possessed." She looked around, like she was looking to see if there was anyone around to hear her, then lowered her voice. "By a *sex ghost*."

There was a moment of silence, real heavy, then Anna spoke.

"Dibs on the rest of the bottle. I'm not drunk enough for this."

We're Gonna Need More Wine

"The fuck is a *sex ghost*?" I asked, not bothering to hide my frustration.

"I don't fucking know, you tell me! You're supposed to be the expert on all this weird shit!" Lidda made an effort to cover her kid's ears as she cussed, but that was a lost cause.

"Ghosts, yeah, I know about. I don't normally fuck with 'em, though. And one damn sure ain't never tried to fuck *me!*"

"They'd better not have," Anna muttered, pouring herself another mug.

"Well, then, I don't know what's going on. But it's fucking weird!"

Pinching the bridge of my nose in a vain attempt to ward off the stupidity surrounding me, I sighed. "Why don't you just tell me what's happening, and we can take it from there?"

"Well, ok. So, I guess you heard my Gran-Gran died?"

I hadn't, actually, and that made me a little sad. I'd always liked Charlotte; she didn't take no shit. She was off-the-boat German, and she'd been proper pissed at Lidda when she and I broke up all those years ago. "Damn, I'm sorry. I hadn't."

"Yeah, cancer. About five months ago. I had moved in to help look after her there toward the . . ." She pawed at eyes with the back of her hand. "But, uh . . . so, when she passed, she left me her house."

"The one out on the Shores?" A few decades back, someone had dammed up Catowala Creek and created a small lake. The proper name was Camelia Shores Lake, but everyone just called it the Shores. It was the tiny poor man's version of Lake Martin, all lined with lake houses, mostly, but it was pretty nice all the same.

"Yeah. And you know how she had those rentals, right?"

I did, indeed. Shady Cove Mobile Estates was a really fancy name for six small mobile homes barely more than campers arranged in a half circle around a small lagoon.

But that was how Charlotte kept herself going on three packs a day of Virginia Slims and bottom-shelf brandy.

In retrospect, maybe her death wasn't *that* unexpected.

"Yeah. They ain't rusted slam apart yet?"

Lidda looked affronted. "Excuse you. Gran-Gran kept them in great shape."

"The Sex Ghost of the Shores," Anna giggled from the couch.

Lidda rolled her eyes. "Glad this is all *so funny* to you."

"Zip!" I said, snapping my fingers. "Focus, 'cause if I gotta risk losing my buzz to hear this, you gotta come correct. So where's the ghost?"

"Oh, God forbid you spend half a second not blitzed out of your gourd."

She was starting to press my buttons. "Put up with shit like this your whole life and then come talk to me about what gets me through the day. I seem to recall you not having any complaints all those times you sucked on my glass."

"Is that, like, a sex phrase? You know what, I don't wanna know." Anna shook her head even as she said it.

"Oh, climb down off the cross, Marsh, we need the wood," Lidda spat.

"That's *definitely* a sex phrase," Anna mumbled into her mug.

I should have rolled my door shut the moment Lidda had pulled up. Or maybe just shot myself and put myself out of my misery. "Fuck me. Lidda. What. Is. Happening?!"

"All the old folks are acting weird as hell. Like, real fucking weird. And they used to not be, but now they are."

I was lost again. "The old folks?"

"Yeah, the renters. They're all over fifty, at least. Most of them have been renting there, like, since we were teens. They used to be normal, and now they aren't."

"Ok … did this start when Charlotte died?" Maybe the old folks were acting out now that the indomitable Charlotte was out the picture, I figured.

Lidda shook her head. "What? Oh, no. It started about three weeks ago. They went from normal, churchgoing old folks to, like, skinny-dipping, streaking sex fiends."

"… What?"

"I've seen things, Marsh. Things no one should ever have to see." A haunted look crept into her eye, and I saw her shudder a little.

"I mean, maybe they just—"

"No," Lidda cut me off. "You don't understand. The things I have seen, it ain't natural. These folks are acting like they're possessed with a sex ghost or something. So, I need you to come over and do whatever it is you do, and get my renters back to normal."

"I mean, Viagra has done wonders for old people sex. Maybe they just—" Anna tried to say.

"*No*. This ain't Viagra in the water. This is old people having a goddamn orgy on the roof of a mobile home wearing nothing but goddamn moonlight! Poor Mrs. Goddrick broke her leg climbing down, and I had to be the one to talk to the paramedics and try to explain why the hell a seventy-year-old woman was up on the roof buck naked."

"Oof" was all I could think to say.

"Do you know how many saggy old balls I've seen in the past three weeks? More than anyone should ever, EVER, have to see. I have nightmares now where I hear them slapping against their thighs as they chase me along the shore. Do you have even an *inkling* of how bad that is?!"

"Jesus," Anna whispered, eyes wide. I could tell she was picturing it, and she didn't like what she saw.

"A'aight," I said after a second or two of thought. This certainly didn't sound normal. I really didn't tend to fuck with ghosts much—that was more the domain of a buddy of mine, Jeff Earl. But I figured I could at least go take a look, and iff'n it was ghosts, we could get him on the case.

I could see a little tension drain from Lidda's shoulders. "So you'll come out and take care of it? Tonight? It's always worse on the weekends, so you should see a lot of evidence or whatever."

"Well, the weekends is when I spend time with—"

Anna cut me off. "We'll be over as soon as I'm sober enough to drive."

So that was that.

You Fool, It's Only Moonlight

The thing about Anna being sober enough to drive was that it meant I could keep drinking. While I slowed things down a bit, I certainly didn't stop. There was fuckery afoot, and it wouldn't do to face it sober.

The other thing about Anna being sober enough to drive was that she wasn't done drinking just then. I think she was of a similar mind and wasn't really committed to the idea of drying out her liver. So, we finished up that wine, just like we'd planned, and only then did she stop drinking.

So, suffice it to say it was a good few hours after Lidda left that we finally got on the road. And then, of course, we had to detour over to the Waffle House, because that's what you do when you're drunk, or just getting over being drunk. Because nothing battles a hangover better than coffee and a big ol' plate of greasy hash browns.

Feeling properly fat and sassy now, we rolled up to the Shores at about five o'clock. Through the window, I could see the lake off to my right as we toddled up Highway 23. It was a large expanse of blue-brown water that stretched out at least a good mile into the distance. The sun was still fairly high up, and its reflection made the waves look almost like they were tipped with lines of white-hot electricity. It contrasted beautifully with the shaded alcoves lined with tall pines. They looked mighty inviting, just begging for someone to take a dip in them.

You go up to Lake Martin, and you drive past million-dollar homes lining the lake in most places. The Shores didn't have anything on that level, but it did have more than its fair share of nice houses. There wasn't a trailer in sight, and most every home you saw was kept up nicely, with tidy little yards and the like. I knew a lot of these were more like vacation places and weekend getaways for the few folks in the County that had money, but I'd guess that a bit more than half of these were actually full-time residences.

And fuck me if everyone didn't have a boat or two, from the looks of things. I, for one, never saw the appeal in owning a boat. I get the appeal of riding in a boat, sure, but actually owning one? Fuck that. Two happiest days in a boat owner's life are the day they buy it and the day they sell it, Granddaddy had always told me, and I took that to heart.

I mean, not that I had ever actually had enough money to buy a boat. But if I had, you can bet your ass I wouldn't. Especially not if every one of my neighbors had one.

We crossed a bunch of little bridges, each one traveling over either one of the creeks that fed the lake or some sort of inlet. The longest one was the Kerry Creek Bridge, a good hundred feet of concrete that came before the closest thing the Shores had to a town. It didn't really have a name that I knew of, though I'm sure the Shores-ites probably had given it one. Nameless as it was, it was just a wide part in the road that had a gas station, a small restaurant that I always wondered how it survived, a bait shop, and a small engine repair and boat sales kinda place. I'd never had a reason to stop here, but I knew it meant we were getting close.

A mile past the bridge, the road pulled away from the shore a bit. There was a tree-covered spit of land there that jutted out into the lake like a thumb to our right, and that was where we needed to be. Pointing out the purple mailboxes that marked the driveway to Anna, we slowed and then turned in. There were seven mailboxes all set on sturdy cross slab of wood, each the same garish purple they had been back when I was last out this way a decade or more ago.

The driveway split in two about thirty yards up and I gestured for us to take the right fork, which drifted steadily upwards. The left would take you down to the lagoon and the rentals, while the right went up the little hill where Charlotte's old house was. Where Lidda would hopefully be, or else I was gonna be real pissed.

The drive was mostly dirt, with just a hint of the gravel it had once been sticking through in places. Long ago the grass along the sides would have been cut, but now it was mostly just weeds and shrubs filling the space between the drive and the trees. Most of the spit was covered pretty thickly with those same tall pine trees that lined much of the rest of the lake, thick enough you could only see hints of the water through those shaded boughs.

About halfway up, the trees to our left thinned a little and you could see a few flashes of color, mostly pastels and teals. Those were the rentals, though there were still enough trees to keep you from getting a real good look at them. I knew we would be seeing them soon enough anyway, so I didn't try too hard to catch a glimpse yet, just pointing them out to Anna.

If you didn't know this place was in Alabama, you'd think it was in Maine or some shit. I say that, having never been to Maine . . . but I've read books and seen pictures. Probably seen a movie set there, too. I know what it's supposed to look like, is my point, and this place was like what I imagined Maine would be like.

I was about to say so just then when I thought I saw a tall figure of what appeared to be a man standing among the trees, watching us. But the moment I looked closer, they vanished behind a tree. I jerked my head around to try and see them again, but I couldn't see shit but shadow and pine.

"What?" Anna asked, slowing a little.

I kept looking but didn't see whoever it was again. "Think I saw someone standing out there in the woods."

"Lidda?"

"Naw," I said, giving up on looking. "Probably one of the renters."

"Were they naked?" Anna asked with a laugh.

I laughed at that, and the tension bled out of me a little. "No. Guess it's not party time yet."

We rounded the last little curve, and the clearing that held Lidda's home came into view. It was a nice little one-story wood-paneled building. It was painted a dark-blue color with obnoxious red shudders around the windows. Charlotte had an unnatural love of color, and clearly Lidda hadn't gotten around to painting the place something decent, or just stripping the paint off altogether. I ain't no designer, but I think a nice wood building set back among these pines would look nice.

A broad covered front porch lined the front of the house. A few rockers and a nice swing dotted it, as well as a couple of hanging ferns. The decor gave the house a sleepy look, like the whole place was ready to just nod off and take a nap. I was feeling that way myself, being full of a triple order of hash browns scattered well, covered, and chunked.

Lidda's beater was parked under an awning, which also had an equally old minivan parked underneath. Another remnant of Charlotte's, I reckoned. Her touch was heavy on the ground of this place, too, from the yard full of flowers and shrubs to a disturbing number of lawn ornaments. And while the driveway had been more or less left to its own devices, from the looks of things, Lidda had been making an effort to keep up the yard. Which, frankly, seemed very un-Lidda-like.

Behind the house, the pines had been cleared away, and you could see the lake pretty as you please. I knew there was a set of wooden steps that led down to a small dock, though where we parked, you couldn't quite see them. But the view really was something else.

Lidda and I had quite the history between us, more good than bad, really. But I had to say, I was happy for her. She'd probably fuck it up, but for now at least she had a good thing going. It just sucked that Charlotte had to die for it to happen. But then that's the way of things, I guess.

Anna came to a stop in the middle of the circle drive, halfway between a statue of a pantsless gnome mooning a statue of a turkey and the blindingly red front door. Red doors are supposed to mean something, but at that moment I couldn't remember just what. Safety? Danger? Fuck, who knows. At least she hadn't painted the place up in haint blue; I'd grown to hate that fucking color.

I stepped out of the car just as Lidda came through the door onto the porch. "Took y'all long enough, didn't it?"

I should have just gotten back in the car right then.

So, to Each Their Own

I'll admit it, I was hiding. Sorta.

Things got fucky for me when Lidda refused to let me bring any smokes or drugs into the house. I was wanting to have a little toke, and I knew I would probably need to "fill up my tank" to deal with all this, so to speak. But fuck me if she hadn't got fully clean. Watching Charlotte die seemed to have had a real effect on her, and she'd managed to kick a litany of bad habits. Said all she ever did anymore was have a beer or two, or maybe a bottle of wine.

I mean, she'd never even been close to as deep into it as I was. Like Anna, she had mostly steered clear of the harder stuff, at least unless I was around. I guess all them kids kept her a little more on the straight and narrow than me. Regardless, my box of oblivion and smokes were forbidden from coming into the house.

That's when the cold knife of betrayal plunged deep into my back: Anna had gone on in the house with Lidda to go halfsies on some box wine. That was all the sign I needed to stay far away, because no good was gonna come from those two having a drink together. Either they'd end up fighting, which I didn't want to be around, or they would end up best fucking friends, which I *damn sure* didn't want to be around. Last thing in this world I wanted was my girlfriend and my ex sitting around discussing my endless number of failings.

So, I'd bypassed the house completely and made my way around to the back. There was a nice playset there, far better than anything Lidda had had back at her old place, but I had my eye on the dock. Even if the swing set did look inviting.

A dozen steps got me down onto the small dock, a strip of boards about ten feet wide and twice again as long. Most importantly, it still had the same old bench I remembered. It was metal, and solid as hell. I'd never met Charlotte's husband, and couldn't even begin to try and remember his name, but I knew he'd been a welder. He'd made the bench to last, and last it had. A sun-bleached set of those outdoor cushions made it tolerable to spend some time on, so that's what I did.

The sun was a little lower on the horizon now, and I knew that in about an hour or so I would get to enjoy a show as the sun set. And between my box and my beer,

I intended to be ready for it. So, setting everything down within arm's reach, I took my seat and decided to Zen out and ignore whatever was going on in the house behind me.

The Shores didn't have the size of the bigger lakes, but that didn't mean it was any less pretty. I sprawled out there, sipping beer and rolling up a joint, and just enjoyed the view. A couple of boats were puttering about out there—fishers, from the looks of things, mostly not having any luck that I could see. But then I guess that's why they call it "fishing" and not "catching."

Time seemed to move like syrup. It was warm, but not hot, and the breeze coming up off the water felt damn good. It reminded me of some of the happier days of my youth, way back when Lidda and I had been an item. In fact, she gave me my first dry tugger one early winter day on this very dock, moving carefully beneath the blanket we had tossed across our laps in case Charlotte came wandering down.

They'd had a boat back in those days—just a little jon boat without even a trolling motor—but I took it out a few times, paddling around until my arms were tired. Charlotte took us out once or twice, too, and she even let me have a sip or two of beer—nothing too crazy. We'd done a little fishing but mostly just hung out and listened to her stories about life back in Germany when she was a kid.

For someone who'd never even thought about leaving the state, much less the country, they were crazy interesting.

So yeah, all in all, it was nice. A little trip down memory lane, at least through the good neighborhoods, while getting to take in a little sunshine and good weather was a nice way to pass some time. I probably should have been up in the house learning the lay of the land, but frankly I really didn't want to know. It would come in time, or it wouldn't. For now, I was gonna avoid work and chill.

A small splash caught my attention and my gaze drifted to the left, over into the lagoon. It was too dark to see what caused it. I reckoned it was just a bass or maybe a big frog and was about to go back to my one-man party when I saw a faint glow beneath the surface of the water. It was hard to see it at first due to the reflection of the setting sun, but the closer it got, the more it became clear that something was there. And it weren't no submarine.

Two large round eyes the size of big dinner plates, glowing a pale blue-white, were gazing out at me. They were maybe a dozen feet out into the water, slowly coming in my direction. They were ever so gently swaying from side to side, likely from the thing swimming like a fuck-off-big fish, I guessed.

Not that I was doing a whole lot of thinking. I stood up, ready to run; I didn't even bother trying to summon up my power. Father Flathead was so far beyond me in power that if he really wanted to, he could just squash me like a bug.

That big head of his broke the surface maybe five feet from the shore, right in the middle of some lily pads and cattails, and they parted for him like a boot through grass. I started backing up, not daring to take my eyes off the giant catfish. As it surfaced, the glow of its eyes faded, leaving two jet-black circles gazing back at me. They were cold, lifeless things.

"*Soon*" echoed in my mind. It filled my head like the boom of a cannon, heavy with the weight of endless centuries and incredible power. It reverberated through me, leaving me feeling all tingly.

I squeaked. I staggered back a step, which caused me to trip over the bench and fall right back into sitting. There wasn't any way I could scrabble over that bench without looking away, and there wasn't enough meth in Jubal County to get me to so much as glance away from the eldritch critter looming up out of the drink.

His mouth was wide enough to just about swallow me whole. His skin had an ancient, leathery look to it, a brown darker than the water on top that faded to a bone white on the underside. The whiskers, a half dozen on each side, were about as thick as my wrist. Unlike a normal catfish, they writhed more like tentacles than conventional whiskers. I wasn't in range just yet, but a couple looked almost like they were reaching out for me.

Father Flathead acted like he was waiting for something. So, I nodded my head in understanding. Because, I mean, what the hell else could I do?

Without leaving so much as a ripple, the massive head sunk back beneath the water. A heartbeat later the giant catfish had vanished, leaving me alone once again. Well, alone if you don't count the heart attack that had come to join me.

I thought about getting up and going inside, but honestly, if Father Flathead had wanted to harm me, he would have. I was safe enough for the moment. And besides, beer and a joint was exactly what I needed to calm my nerves, and both of those things were there beside me. I started with the beer.

Maybe ten minutes later, the sun was drawing close to the horizon, and I heard a door shut back behind me. I didn't bother turning to look, just kept staring out over the water, trying to keep my eyes peeled for any other mystical shenanigans just in case. The few boats had mostly made their way back to their docks, the fish winning the battle that day.

I heard shoes on the wood of the dock, and a few moments later a pair of hands ran themselves over my shoulders and down my chest. A second later, Anna kissed my fore-head. "Enjoying the view?"

"Gettin' better every second," I said, meaning every word. I patted the sun-bleached cushions of the bench. "Come have a sit here beside me."

I cleared off the beer that was left to give her a place to sit down. As she sat, I fired up the joint and took a good long toke. Holding the smoke in, I passed the weed to Anna. "She's not as bad as I thought," she said as she lifted the joint to her lips.

I just snorted, but I felt the tension I had been holding in my shoulders finally start to melt away.

We talked about a whole lot of nothing for a bit, mostly just holding hands and watching the sunset. The sky turned a riot of colors, all reds and purples, and the water took on a beautiful sheen. You didn't get views like this out my shed, that was for sure.

It was a perfect moment.

I've Been Wandering in the Dark About as Long as Sin

"You remember how to get over there without getting lost?" Lidda asked from the porch.

I did, so I just nodded. It was getting pretty dark, but not so much that she couldn't see that. "Anna, you gonna hang back here, right?"

"Sure." We'd talked about it on the way over and decided that even if it was just some sort of weird sex magic, it was still magic, and it would probably be best if she stayed pretty well clear of it. She gave me a quick kiss, then stepped up onto the porch beside my ex.

Lidda looped her arm through Anna's and smiled. "We'll have us a little girls' night while you go fix this shit."

"Jesus," I muttered, turning away from the house. I was gonna regret this night, I just knew it.

I was feeling pretty alright, though. We'd had a good time watching the sunset, real peaceful-like, then we'd wandered back up to the house. After stashing my worst habits back in the car, we were let in the house, which I found was like a damn time capsule. Near as I could tell, the only thing Lidda had changed was adding her kids' toys; otherwise, it was still the little German cabin I remembered, complete with the dozen or so Cuckoo Clocks. They were creepy back then and they were creepy now, so I just made a point to look pretty much anywhere else.

Lidda had filled me in on more of the details as we walked, and I was pretty sure there was something like a succubus at work. I mean, I'd never encountered one before, but HD had talked about them at length. The man was a bona fide encyclopedia when he wanted to be, and I was not for the first time wishing I had paid more attention to him. I knew my magical critters far better than I knew my spellwork, but at the end of the day I was still me, so that was a low bar. I had even thought about calling him, but I didn't want one of his lectures to harsh my mellow, so I'd said fuck it. I knew how to handle demons, and that's basically what a succubus was anyhow.

I stepped onto the path that led to the trailers. It was basically just a footpath, about two people wide and worn deep into the hillside from decades of folks walking it. I had a flashlight, but I was trying to go in a little sneaky, and it was bright enough that I decided I would just do without. I wished I had Horace there with me, but Anna had straight up told me no. The fact he was basically my magical battery pack apparently meant jack shit, since there was no way she was gonna allow him to be put in harm's way. Me? Sure. The fucking possum? No, not our sweet prince!

Not being in any real hurry I took my time, keeping my eyes peeled. Now that I was out here alone, I got to thinking about the figure I had seen earlier. What if whoever that had been was still lurking out here? It sorta gave me the heebie-jeebies, and I was getting that prickly feeling of being watched.

I stopped for a second, peering into the woods around me. There was a good-sized moon up, sure, but that doesn't do a whole lot when you're traipsing through a passel of thick pine boughs. I mostly ended up just listening, trying to hear if anything was rustling around out there.

There wasn't anything moving around that I could see, but I thought for a moment I might have heard something. It was like something had been walking in step with me, then not realized I had stopped moving until they had taken a step or two more, but it could also have just been a squirrel or something. I'm not Daniel Boone here. Other than that one quick little sound, all I could hear was the faint sound of water lapping against the shore and the trill of some night bird.

Sufficiently creeped out, I started back walking. I sorta walked slow and made a few more pauses to see if whatever it was out there would mess up and make some more noise, but either it got smarter or my usual level of drug-fueled paranoia was to blame for my earlier suspicions. I couldn't shake the feeling of being followed, but I managed to hold it together well enough.

After about a hundred feet, the path, which had been generally trending downwards, reached the shore. From there I could see that it followed the waterline until it reached the nearest of the trailers. For the first time, I could see them clearly—at least as clearly as you can in the dark, that is.

There were six of them arrayed in a half circle around the lagoon-like spur of the lake. The mouth of the water was maybe fifty yards across, and I reckon it was about half again as deep, flowing up toward the road a bit. There was a pretty good crop of cattails and marsh grasses along the sides of it, broken in a few places by a few ancient wooden docks. There were no boats tied up to them, but more than a few battered lawn chairs were dotted around, no doubt there to provide perches for fishing.

The trailers were small and old, but even in the moonlight you could see the paint jobs they had. They were all done up in what I always thought of as Florida colors: pinks and teals. It was like a tornado had sucked up a trailer park from some sandy South Florida beach and then dropped it right here on the Shores. They had been old a decade ago, so I knew they would only be more so now. The paint had always been kept up fresh, though, so that sorta hid the worst of it.

I could see more than a few potted plants and lawn ornaments in the small squares of light coming from the windows. It was like a greenhouse and a family of gnomes and flamingoes had screwed and made a fucked-up bevy of kids, then hurled them all across the small yards. It actually sorta felt real homey to me; it was like someone had tipped over my shed and spread out all the random crap across a whole-ass yard, but more green.

As I stood there, I heard a cackle of laughter and saw a door open across the way. An older couple was spilling out of the trailer on the far end, stepping out onto the porch with a torrent of giggles. I was pretty sure they were holding martini glasses in one hand, and the guy had a cooler in his other. My eyes were instantly drawn to the bewildering array of colors that constituted the impeccable Hawaiian shirt the man had on, and I was instantly jealous. I loved a good Hawaiian.

I stepped back more into the shadowed tree line and decided to just play reconnaissance for a bit. Everyone had on their clothes, for which I was thankful, so it didn't look like the sort of shenanigans that Lidda had been going on about. But you never know when things might pop off, so I was in spy mode.

It suddenly occurred to me that if they were gonna get naked, and I was watching, and they caught me, I would probably be going to jail for being a Peeping Tom. For a moment, the thought sprung into my head that maybe nothing was going on and Lidda was setting me up. Old people could be swingers without magic being involved . . . in fact, that was far, far more likely a scenario.

My mind started frantically thinking back to my most recent interaction with Lidda prior to this fuckery. It had been awhile, for sure, but I was pretty sure I hadn't done anything. Hell, I think we'd even slept together, but I wasn't real sure on that. Was she thinking we were gonna get back together? Surely not, right? She'd been with . . . hell, I couldn't even remember who she'd been with then, but there had definitely been a guy in the picture.

It was nothing out of the ordinary for us, but maybe I'd done something I didn't remember? I decided to be extra cautious just in case. I didn't think she'd set me up, but hell, who knew?

The couple had made it to their closest neighbors, and they took to smacking the end of the trailer as they passed by. They whooped and hollered something, but they were far enough away and facing away from me, so I couldn't make out just what they said. It sounded like it might be names.

I watched as they went from trailer to trailer, banging and shouting away. By the time they reached one of the closest trailers to me, folks were beginning to trickle out of the others. There was an older lady by herself, and then another two sets of couples. All of them looked to be a good bit over the hill, and they mostly moved with that sort of stiffness that comes with advanced age. It was too dark to make out exactly, but gun to my head, I'd guess that the youngest was probably in their late fifties. The woman by herself, who was pretty heavyset, was rolling an oxygen tank behind them in one hand, holding a fuck-off-big thermos in the other.

Standing where I was, I lost sight of everyone pretty quickly as they reached the next-to-nearest trailer to me. They all had been going along in the backyards, just skirting the edge of the lagoon, and that meant they were on the wrong side of that trailer for me to be able to see them. I could definitely hear them, though. Sounded like it was shaping up to be quite a party.

I could see the water behind that trailer start reflecting a whole lot of light of a sudden. It looked like a whole mess of stars maybe, so my best guess was someone had just cut on a bunch of string lights. It's just not a top-level outdoor party without either a bonfire or string lights, if you ask me, and clearly these folks had the same sort of mindset.

I noticed that the trailer closest to me was seemingly being left alone. I'd have thought maybe no one was home, or maybe it wasn't currently being rented, but there was one light on that I could clearly see. A lamp, from the looks of things, though at my current distance I couldn't be sure. It seemed to me that someone was either an outcast or just not up for a party. Regardless, I figured that made for a little opening I could take advantage of.

I waited a few minutes to make sure no one was going to come around to the front. When no one did, I began sneaking along the tree line toward the nearest trailer. The laughter wasn't as loud now—I guess folks were settling in a little—but I could still hear them talking in that overly loud manner drunk people are wont to do.

When I got close enough, I left the shelter of the trees and scuttled over to the corner of the trailer. Now that I was close enough, I could see it was painted a bright teal, and not the gray the moonlight had made it look from a distance. And I could also see that yep, these trailers were *old*, and pretty damn small—nothing like the behemoths they churned out these days.

I crept over to the window where I had seen the lamp. Being reeeeal slow and careful, I took a little peek to see if I could feel out the lay of the land. There was an old man sitting there, his back mostly to me, reading a book. When I saw he had his back turned, I nudged over to get a better look.

This window opened into what I guessed was the living room. Besides the chair, I could see an old TV, which was off, and a little sofa that looked to be older than I was. I couldn't tell what the old man was reading, but he seemed pretty intent on it. He was bald, but the scruff of his beard was white as a ghost, and the tuft of hair coming out the ear I could see was pretty damn prodigious. Most importantly, it looked like he wasn't going anywhere any time soon, so I returned to the end of the trailer.

I skirted down the end of it, taking care to not get tangled up in a water hose that was hanging from an old tire rim. I was now edged up to the lagoon side of the trailer, and I could hear the laughter and chatter more clearly. Hunching down as low as I could get without laying slap down on the ground, I started to ever so slowly peer around the corner. At night, folks were more likely to see my movement rather than me myself, or at least that's what my years of bootleg burglary had proven to me. So I moved molasses slow, super smooth.

There were eight or nine folks either standing or sitting there in the space between the pink trailer and the water. The owners of the pink trailer, which was very much that pale beach condo pink, had built an awning that went the length of their home and covered out to where they had built their little dock. Everyone had plenty of room to lounge about, and there were more than enough chairs. There was even a real nice picnic table right in the middle of it all, and hanging on the far side was a wooden swing where the couple I had first seen had sat themselves.

Everyone was dressed for a beach party, from the looks of things. All the men had on fucking gorgeous Hawaiian shirts, enough to make a man jealous, for sure. The women were mostly wearing floral-print dresses, though one of them looked like she had just stepped off the golf course. Right after I dropped outta school, I was a groundskeeper at the Sumpville Country Club for a week before they fired me for wrecking a golf cart. I was a veritable expert, and she had the look of a lady golfer for sure.

They all had drinks in their hands, and someone had put some sort of fruit tray or something on the table. Not that it was getting much love, that I could see. Why have an orange slice when you can have a tequila sunrise, amirite?

But you know what? Nothing looked the least little bit odd. It was just a bunch of old folks hanging out on a Saturday night. An exceptionally well-dressed bunch, at least on the guy side, but that was only unusual in that you don't expect that much class and sophistication in Jubal County.

I resolved that, alongside my mullet, within the year I would start sporting some nice Hawaiians. I was gonna be goddamn magnificent. Look good, feel good. The only sad thing about it was the fact that any Hawaiian shirt I found at the Christian mission would have come from a dead man, 'cause clearly only death could cause someone to get rid of clothes so fantastic.

Anyway, I watched for a couple of minutes and didn't see anything at all weird. But hey, the night was young. So, I decided to let the liquor do what it does best and see what cropped up. I had nothing but time.

Well, Damn

This may come as a bit of a surprise, but I am not famously patient.

I did pretty good at first, just copping a squat there behind the teal trailer and carefully peeking out every few minutes. It was just a whole lot of drinking, near as I could tell, with folks generally having a good time from the sounds of things.

There was one woman, though, who had a laugh that was slowly killing me. It was like a backfiring lawnmower and a mule were being run through a blender, and worse, it was loud as all hell. And someone over there musta been tickling her funny bone, because she. Just. Kept. Laughing.

It was enough to drive a guy to drinking, only I didn't have anything to drink. I had a joint in my pocket, along with a couple of shrooms and a pill or two. It was one of the things, though, where nothing will do but the thing you want, and I wanted a damn beer. Preferably a Headcrusher or a Natty Daddy. Hell, I'd even have settled for some of the Beast, or a few Stones. Anything, really; I'm no slave to taste.

I started weighing the option of going back up to Lidda's and grabbing a couple of beers to tide me over. Hell, I even had a few fantasies of going full superspy and sneaking over to steal some drinks from the plethora of coolers the old folks had gathered up. I mean, I knew better, but visions of me as a mulleted James Bond sure helped pass the time.

Around then was when I caught a whiff of green. Taking a quick glance, I visually confirmed what my nose was telling me: the old folks had taken out a goddamn hookah. And from the smell of things, I could tell that it wasn't sumbitchin' flavored tobacco they had burning in there. Who has a hookah? In Jubal County, of all places? That's the sort of shit college kids in, like, college towns had—not people on the goddamn Shores.

I was jealous as all hell.

If they were gonna smoke, then by God, so was I. Fishing the joint out of my pocket, I summoned up my lighter from the void. I sorta scooted over closer to the middle of the trailer, deciding that it wouldn't do for them to see smoke coming out from the side where I was. It wasn't likely, sure, but if I was gonna do something dumb, I reckoned I would at least try to be a *little* safe with it.

Flaming up, I took a deep drag, holding the dank air in my lungs. I sputtered out a few small coughs, making an effort to not just go hacking up a storm. Taking it in, I realized it was just what I needed. Every little drag made me a bit more calm, a bit more steady. Planning things out, I decided I would smoke the whole thing, then settle in for the long haul.

It was pretty well full dark at this point, and staring out onto the lake, I could see tiny dots of lights. Some were up in the sky, stars and satellites and shit, but a lot were along the far shore. It was a little like fireflies, only they didn't go winking in and out. I could even see a hint of glow from up the hill where Lidda's house was, even though the trees were too thick for me to see properly.

I was just about down to the roach when I heard the sound of someone pumping a shotgun behind me.

Straight Shooter

"Come on outta there," said a thin, tired voice. The shotgun wasn't raised up at me, but it was held so that it could be in a hurry if needed.

It was the old man, of course. I guess I hadn't been as quiet with my coughing as I thought. Slowly, I stood up straight, my hands raised. I didn't drop the joint, though I was pretty sure that would have been the smart move. But damn it, I ain't one to waste any weed. And if the ol' boy had wanted to shoot me, I reckoned he'd have done it by now. "Easy now," I said, a little cough of smoke coming out as I spoke.

"The hell you doing sneakin' 'round my house?" he said.

Now Lidda had made it really, really clear to me that if anyone caught me, I was in no way, shape, or form to say that I was there because she had asked me to be. She said she had a reputation to maintain with her tenants, and hiring a meth head to dig their nose into shit wouldn't help that one iota. So, I said the only thing I could. "Lidda asked me to."

His eyes narrowed, and he didn't lower the gun. "Lidda asked you to go sneaking around my trailer? What the hell for? I pay my rent on time, in full, in cash, and don't cause no trouble."

"Fuck!" I shouted as the joint burned down to the tips of my fingers, singeing me. It startled me more than hurt me and I dropped the roach. My fingers went to my mouth, but the moisture didn't really help.

None of this set the old man at ease, mind you. It sorta had the opposite effect, in fact, as that gun was now clearly pointed in my direction, which had a real dampening effect on my mood. Carefully, I pulled my fingers out of my mouth and raised my hand again.

I could see the gun shaking slightly in his hands, its weight clearly more than his thin limbs could handle. "Better speak up, son, before I do something we both regret."

"Hey, now . . . take it easy. I ain't here to creep on you or nothing. Lidda, she's, ugh . . . she's got some questions." Fuck it. "Like about the weird shit going on down here. She wants me to take a look for her."

He was still looking hard at me, but he lowered the gun a fraction. "You mean like all them sex parties and shit?"

Bingo. "Exactly. She's worried is all, but she doesn't want to—"

"Creep around in the bushes and spy. So, she sent you." He spat, but he also lowered the gun. "Well, I ain't got much of a high opinion of folks spying, but I appreciate her taking notice. It's plumb got me about to move out."

"Can I . . ." I sorta gestured like lowering my arms. When he nodded, I cautiously put my arms down at my side. "You wanna fill me in? See if I can't maybe help?"

The old man snorted. "Doubt you can, but come on, I don't like to be outside on Saturday nights. And don't you try nothin'."

He slung the shotgun over one shoulder and led me to the door on the front of his trailer. You could see the glow of lights coming from next door, as well as hear the bray of laughter and such. He paused at the door to flip an impotent bird in the direction of the party, which, though I could see was filled with anger, really just came off as sorta petty and pathetic. I kept my mouth shut, though. I mean, he did still have a shotgun in his hands, even if it seemed pretty certain he wasn't gonna pull it on me again.

It smelled like old people inside. Not like that sour, bad smell of someone too old to give a shit about taking a bath, but that sorta stale smell that, while not bad, isn't exactly good. But seeing as he was old, the trailer was old, and all the furniture was old, what did I expect?

As I pulled the door shut behind me, he stalked across the room to the far side and slid a finger between the slats of the blinds. "Don't reckon anyone heard the fuss," he said as he looked out at the folks next door. Letting the blinds flick closed, he straightened up and leaned the gun up against the wall. Turning around, he eyed me up and down. "May as well take a seat," he added, gesturing to the chair I had seen him sitting in earlier as he sat down on the love seat.

"Sure," I said, sitting down and taking in my surroundings. The lamp on the little table beside me was almost painfully bright after hanging out so long in the dark. Beneath it sat the book, left open and face down, next to a mug filled with what looked like some sorta tea. It was some book by Wilbur Smith, who I'd never heard of, though the cover made it clear it wasn't fantasy or sci-fi, so that wasn't exactly a surprise. The chair itself was comfortable, though it didn't quite fit me, having been long since worn into the shape of the old man's ass.

"What's your name, son?"

"Howard Marsh."

"Aight, then. I'm Daryl. I'd offer you something to drink, but I ain't really feeling all that neighborly."

I could relate. "Fair enough. How 'bout you fill me in and I get out your hair?"

"Sounds good. So about two, mebbe three months ago, the Fourtnoys next door came back from vacation. I forget where, 'cause really, ever since my Gertie passed, I ain't been all that social with everyone. And to be honest, I just don't give a shit. I watered their plants for them like they asked, and that shoulda been that." He licked his lips.

He was one of those people that the more they talked, the more they got some, like, mucus buildup in the corners of their mouth. I hated that shit. But I tried my darndest to ignore it, even if my eyes kept drifting back there.

"Only they came back weird. They was all about parties now, having them every Saturday for sure, and normally a night or two during the week. Grillin' shit, playing music, being loud, and just generally getting on my last nerve. They ask me every damn time if I wanna join, and every time I tell them not no, but hell no. We ain't thirty no more. Hell, we ain't fifty no more!"

I didn't plan to live that long, but if by some miracle I did, I reckoned I was gonna be a lot more like the Fourtnoys than Daryl. Least I hoped so. Not that it was likely—I mean, let's be real, it's been a wonder I'd made it this long between the drugs and the mystic shit trying to kill me. Mostly the drugs.

"And I'd have been fine with that. Pissed, sure, but I stay pissed these days, what with what the damn lib'ruls have been doing to America. Commie bastards bringing all them drugs and socialism in from China and Mexico and shit. My daddy didn't lose his leg in the Pacific so that—"

"Reel it in, Daryl," I said, cutting off what was sure to be a Fox News highlight reel.

He frowned and eyed me hard, like he was weighing my potential communist status. Meth ain't a political party last time I checked, so he was barking up the wrong tree there. "So like I said, if it was just cookouts, I'd have been fine with it. But right quick-like, it became a whole hell of lot more than that." He leaned forward and lowered his voice. "They's having sex parties now."

Which is basically what Lidda had told me. And like earlier, there was absolutely nothing about an old-person sex party that was magic in nature. "Ok . . . so how's that weird? I mean, maybe they just got into being swingers on their vacation and got everyone else but you hooked on it."

"Miss Hagar's been the piano player down at the Elk Grove Church of the Redeemer long as I've known her. Tim and Elsie, they take them a mission trip to Panama every winter. Now, the Fourtnoys've always been a little wild—they ain't from Jubal County originally, so I could expect it of them, sure. But the rest of them? Ain't no damn way."

"People change," I said with a shrug. I mean, not usually, but I'd heard it was possible.

"I seen more change in my life than you can imagine, son. I know that. But I also know that ain't no one who plays piano down at the church every Sunday gonna go skinny-dippin' in front of God and the world on Saturday in clear sight of the damn road. I ain't dumb; I know folks get into some weird shit behind closed doors. But I seen, with my own damn eyes, Tim and Elsie doin' it like dogs out there on the damn roof next door, clear as day. The *roof?* How in the hell did they even get up there, 'specially with Tim's hip replacement?! And anyone drivin' by who looked that way woulda seen the same damn thing. Try explaining that to your mission trip buddies."

If there was one thing me and Daryl could probably agree on, it was just how many damn hypocrites there were in Jubal County. And he was right: ain't a one that would want that exposed. Still, church folks bumping uglies in public was pretty far from normal, but it didn't mean magic was at work.

"That makes sense. But some folks are just weird. And all folks are dumb, just about different shit."

He sucked his teeth, clearly weighing something in his mind. He didn't say anything, though, instead just sorta glancing in the direction of the neighboring trailer, as if he could see it through the wall. "Sure, sure," he finally said, clearly unhappy.

I was pretty sure he was hiding something. I had a spell for that maybe, but I needed some way to distract him. "Are they still at it over there?" I asked, hoping to get him to turn and look out the window.

He rolled his eyes. "You can hear them, can't you? All that damn cackling . . . Jesus, it just don't end. Least not till later in the night, when the sex starts happening."

So much for that. Welp, in for a penny, in for a pound. "You think maybe something weirder is going on here than just folks becoming swingers, don't you? Something, like, supernatural or something?"

I ain't no poker player, but the way his right eye twitched said something, I reckoned. "No, 'course not. Ain't no such kinda thing." He started to get up out of his seat. "And I think mebbe it's best you started headin' on. Tell Lidda thanks for taking an interest, but to kindly go on and mind her business, 'less she's planning to kick out the perverts."

Him being old, and more than a little frail, he was having to do that rocking thing that some old folks have to do to get up. Especially when they sit on something a bit softer than they should have, like a nice cushiony couch. It wasn't much, but it was enough.

I started twisting my fingers in the patterns I had learned as a kid. Now that I was learning stuff, I was beginning to suspect that I probably could have learned to do it without the finger moving, but since I had, I was pretty well locked into it mentally. Magic was a little more free-flowing, I was coming to learn, but I guess it had helped child me learn, and old habits die hard. I muttered a few words under my breath, filling them with a trickle of power, and turned the working loose.

"What was that?" he said, getting unsteadily to his feet.

Time to see if it had worked. If he hadn't paused so much earlier, leading me to believe he was thinking on telling me then, I wouldn't have tried it on the ornery old cuss, but it felt like there was enough doubt there to give my spell something to latch on to. "I said, you sure there ain't something supernatural going on?"

He opened his mouth, sorta angry-like, but then closed it. "Ahh hell. Not like you gonna believe me if I tell you," he spat.

"I reckon I'm more of a believin' sort than you'd think."

He eyed me over. "Mebbe so. Look, all I know is, 'bout the time they took up with all this bull mess, there started being some blue lights glowing out their windows. Like what you see on the UFO movies, when folks get ab-ducted. Every time they've gone nuts over there, I've seen them lights. And I know you gotta be thinking, 'Oh, well, it's probably just a blue light bulb or something.' Probably what I would be thinking, too, if I hadn't see it with my own eyes. Ain't no GD bulb, I promise you that."

I nodded, getting to my feet. "Fair enough. You reckon if I hang around late enough tonight, I'll see 'em, too?"

He frowned, but nodded. "Sure. Another hour or two, tops."

"You mind if I go back to my creepin', then? I made Lidda a promise, and I intend to keep it." And then, though it galled me to say it, I added, "She really does want to fix things here, or she wouldn't have sent me. She's pretty aight. Like her granny."

"Got you some sort of alien ray gun of your own, then?" he said with a snort.

"Something like that."

He gave me that same hard look, but in the end he nodded. He started ushering me to the door. "You can't hang out in here. I'mma try to get some damn sleep. But so long as you keep it down, I don't give a damn what you do. Just don't touch any of my stuff."

And before I could really respond, I was back outside, in the dark once more.

A Sumbitchin' Cat Burglar

Despite that warm invitation, I decided that it would probably be best if I gave Daryl a wide berth. I mean, I had no intention of making a ruckus, but then when did I ever? Things just seemed to happen around me sometimes, you know? I'm a bit of a ruckus magnet.

I figured watching from the trailer on the other side of the party trailer would be as good a spot as any, since I wasn't looking to climb up on no roofs. I just had to get over there without being seen. So, slipping over to the tree line once more, I set about making my way as quietly as possible through the trees until I could come out far enough away that no errant partier would spot me.

That "being watched" feeling from earlier came back the moment I stepped into the woods. I tried to look around, see if there was anything there. But after a good thirty seconds that felt like an eternity, I hadn't seen anything moving around out there in the pines. No shadowy figures walking around, no sasquatches, nothing. So, keeping my eyes and ear peeled, I started slipping along again as quietly as I could.

And let's be honest: Even though I was basically sober—I mean, at least for me—my natural sense of balance isn't exactly the best. I'm not clumsy, but I'm damn sure not graceful. Couple that fact with it being dark inside the pines and, well, "quiet" was a relative term.

Thankfully, I could still hear the party popping off pretty good. Being farther away and on the wrong side of the trailer, it was more of a faint wall of noise than anything I could specifically point out. Clearly, though, things were going well over there, fueled by a stunning number of beverages and that hookah.

I managed to not put my eye out on any sticks and such, and I also managed to not make such a racket that anyone came calling. I sat there on the edge of the woods for a bit, just watching, making sure that no one was making their way out of the circle of light to drain the lizard or such. I figured everyone would be far too night-blind to have a chance of spotting me so long as I didn't get too close, so once I felt safe, I moved my way across the empty expanse of ground toward the trailer I had settled on to be my new watch post.

There was a patch of earth that was probably meant to be a yard, but it was hard to tell where the yard might start compared to just the regular ol' grass and such. There was an aged maroon Oldsmobile that looked like the color of an old scab parked on a small concrete pad with a little awning overhead. I made for that, using its bulk to help cover me until I was right up against the trailer.

On a hunch, I made my way over to the front door. I gave the handle a try, and sure enough, it opened right up. I weighed things: I could watch from around the corner of the building . . . or I could watch from inside. Watching from outside was risky, as it was easier for me to be seen, but watching from inside was riskier on account of, well, me being inside someone's house without their permission.

A heartbeat later I was walking inside, moving slow and easy. I had been making a real effort to be less criminal of late, outside of the drugs, of course. But my days of breaking and entering were recent enough that none of those skills and inclinations had had time to atrophy. Not that opening an unlocked door was exactly safecracking, mind you.

Stepping in, I paused and stood in silence, barely breathing. Houses have a feel to them that's different if someone else is inside. I don't know how to explain it, and maybe I'm just crazy. Probably I'm just crazy. But I can tell if someone is inside with me more times than not. And this place had that still, quiet feel to it. Confident I was alone, I started easing my way around.

This place was fucking cluttered, which was less than ideal. I could see a little; there was a touch of light coming in through the windows, but there was shit everywhere. It wasn't quite like my level of hoarding, but it made it damn hard to move around without knocking shit over. I bumped into something at one point that made that tinkling sound of ceramic on glass. No doubt some kind of curio cabinet filled with some sort of stomach-churning porcelain knickknacks filling it up.

I never knew my mom's mom. And Granny, she wasn't exactly the doll type, unless they were of the voodoo variety. Her cabinets were more likely to have jars and skulls than pastel-tinted statues of saccharine sweet kids. But I'd been to more than my fair share of estate sales and such, so I knew the type. There was some old lady what lived here, and she had a taste for kitsch.

They also had a taste for cigarettes, by the smell of it. This place damn sure didn't smell like old folks—it smelled like an ashtray. I felt right at home. With my eyes closed, I could almost imagine I was back in my shed, surrounded by my junk.

Making my way through a small tidy kitchen, I found myself in the bedroom. It was just the spot I needed, with a good-sized window across the back of the room above the bed. It had some curtains, but the blinds were goobered up enough that I wouldn't have to crack them myself to watch out.

The bed wasn't too high up, so I moved to step onto it. The moment my foot touched down, though, I pitched forward, falling onto the bed with a muffled shout of surprise. It was a goddamn waterbed. Who the fuck still has one of those?

Someone hadn't made the bed, so in trying to get up I got tangled in some sort of crochet knit thing. It was like a goddamn net, and I was a fucking dolphin. It was like trying to punch my way out of the makeup-caked embrace of an aunt at a family reunion, which just pissed me off, so I ended up thrashing around even more, which in the end did manage to free me, but it probably took at least three times as long.

Panting, pissed, and a little seasick, I crawled across the bed, trying not to think about just how much old people sex remnants were rubbing against me. There was a mantle across the back that held a little alarm clock and what looked like a stack of romance novels beside a lamp. I used the wood of it to steady myself, and after taking a breath I tried to center myself. It didn't really work, since I was basically still panting.

Leaning forward, I peered out through one of the cracks in the blinds. Thanks to the way in which the trailers were lined up in relation to each other, each being more curved in order to make a half circle, I had a good line of sight into most of the backyard where the party was happening. It gave me a much better view than what I'd had earlier. At least my travails had paid off.

The party was moving apace. Folks were getting a little more handsy, from the looks of things. It wasn't anything inappropriate, *yet*, but folks were being a little overly touchy—hands lingering too long on arms, that sort of thing. And while sure, the space wasn't all that large, there wasn't any call for anyone to be standing quite so close to each other.

Seeing everyone a little bit closer up, I could now see more clearly just how old some of them were. I'd been a bit generous in my guess before, as I'd be damn surprised if any of them were under sixty. And the old lady with the oxygen tank was probably pushing seventy, but despite the medical device she kept puffing on, she had clearly once been a mighty stout woman. I'd thought she had been overweight earlier, and she probably was, but she was also just . . . big. And sorta intimidating looking.

They had themselves a whole lot of drinks, and damn if I didn't want one. I decided that since nothing was happening right that second, I would risk a quick looksee in the fridge. Maybe my hosts had some sippin' liquor, or a couple of beers. I mean, what the hell kind of stakeout is it if you don't have something to help get your mind right?

I launched the good ship Howard Marsh across the bed, managing to not capsize myself this time. When I was naught but a little shit, my folks had had a waterbed, up until Black Tom emptied his revolver into it during a drunken fit. Duct tape can't do shit, really, for .45 holes. Luckily, my mom hadn't been in the bed at the time. Though, considering the hell my pa had put her through, maybe it would have been better if she had.

Hell, maybe *I'd* have been better off to have been in there.

With that cheerful thought running through my mind, I opened the fridge. I heard the pleasing rattle of bottles clinking together as I did so, and I was overjoyed to find most of a sixer of Coors bottles. I decided to not be greedy and to just grab one for the moment. One quick twist later, I was slurping down some nice cold beer, and suddenly all was right with the world.

I leaned there against the fridge, taking a few slow sips and just sorta thinking about nothing. The beer was cool on my throat, and I decided to pair it with a smoke. Not like they would notice it amongst the heavy scent already in the air. So, setting the beer down, I pulled out a mostly empty pack of smokes from my back pocket. It was sorta crushed from my bed debacle, but it looked like none of them had broken, so that was ok. With a flick of my wrist,

I magicked up my lighter from the void, lit the smoke, and then magiked it away once more.

As I worked my little snippet of magic, I felt a curious little tickle. This was far and away the most useful, yet tiniest magic I could work, one that I had performed many thousands of times over the years. *Many* thousands. And not once had I ever felt anything like that happen.

It felt . . .

Ok, bear with me. In the strictest sense, it felt like a little rumble of electricity in my fingertips, just a light brush. But what flashed into my mind was a very different sort of thing. For a split fucking second I had a vision of some blind, snuffling thing—a thing of foul air on acrid wings, sniffing its way around like some sort of hunting bird. It was a thing of darkness, of the spaces between, and for a moment I was SEEN.

Nope. Didn't like that one bit.

I tried to chalk it up to some of my usual acid flashbacks or the like, but it didn't want to be discounted so easily. It felt tangible, like I had brushed up against an electric fence and was remembering how it felt. Needless to say, I didn't magic my lighter back away; I just tucked it in my pocket.

Feeling pretty shook, I decided to finish this beer over on the bed, where I could see things a little better. I knew for sure now that something was up, something having to do with magic. And if things didn't start to clear up a bit, well, I had some spells and shrooms for that.

I was just stepping into the bedroom when I heard the lakeside screen door of the trailer go creaking open.

A Thin Chew of Tobacco

F ast? Son, you ain't seen fast till you saw me sprint across that bedroom for the little closet door I could see.

I couldn't hear shit because of the panicked beating of my heart, so I don't know how quiet I really was. The door to the closet didn't seem to have anything too wrong with it where it would make a noise, but I was sorta flinging it open and shut pretty fast. Which is truly a feat when you have a beer in one hand and a lit smoke in the other.

Surrounded by a mess of clothes on hangers, which smelled like mothballs and old people, I warred with what to do with my cigarette. Last thing I needed was to set some polyester suit on fire with an errant cherry, but damned if I wasn't getting low. I thought about trying to put it out with my tongue, but if that went sideways I might gasp or something. So, cursing up a blue streak a mile long in my head, I dropped it into the hardly drank-from beer can. The sound of it hissing to death hurt my soul.

I heard some muted conversation in the living room, followed by a rumbling bark of laughter. There were at least two people, one female, one male, if I had to guess from the tone of the voices. Through the thin walls I could still hear the party going on outside, so I knew things hadn't wrapped up. So why the hell had these folks come home?

It sounded like someone was getting into the fridge maybe—that much, I thought I could hear. But a little softer than that, I was certain that someone else was coming back into the bedroom. Fear gripping my heart tighter than a noodled catfish, I tried to sink as far into the closet as I could.

That ended up not being very far at all, seeing as this was a tiny-ass closet in a tiny-ass trailer. It was about as deep as the width of a sports coat. My back was flat against the wall and I was sure that anyone who opened the door would see me no problem. My feet felt like they were caught up in a cluster of shoes and shit, which meant I couldn't really move around much without making a racket. I tried hunching down a little bit, as much as I could, and tried leaning into the corner. Being short, I had to hope that maybe, if no one looked too close, they'd miss me.

A spread of muffled words from the kitchen was answered by a slightly slurred woman's voice in the bedroom. "Yeah, grab me one, please, dear. You want the big towel?" More words followed from a room away, and suddenly there was a thin sliver of light eking into the closet as she turned on the bedroom light.

It sounded like she was at the foot of the bed, most likely, which meant she couldn't be more than a few feet away from me. I stopped breathing, thinking the smallest thoughts I could. I tried to will myself invisible, which I was pretty sure was possible in some way with magic, but fucked if I knew how. I was having to make do with praying and thinking the tiniest, thinnest thoughts.

Moving around in a trailer like that, you not only hear the footsteps, but if you're close enough you also feel them. The floor sorta groans with each step, and that's exactly what I was feeling as she walked toward the closet. I tried to hunch even lower and smaller, but I was already at my limit of what I could muster in the small space without making some noise or falling over.

I was momentarily blinded as the closet door opened and light came streaming in. It wasn't full-on, since I had a good bit of clothing between me and the door, but enough that I knew it wouldn't take but a moment of looking to see me. My butthole puckered so tight that I could have ate coal and shit a diamond.

The woman standing there was pulling her dress up over her head, revealing that she was wearing not much of anything beneath it other than a pair of, in this case, literal granny panties. The dress slipping over her head was obscuring her vision, but to be fair, I wasn't exactly staring at her face. Time and gravity had put in some work, but at the end of the day I'm still a guy.

She turned slightly and called over her shoulder in response to something. "You had best be folding those clothes neatly over the chair and not just tossing them on the floor!" She went to place the dress in her hand neatly on the bed, turning her back mostly to me.

With a roll of her head, it looked like she was trying to work out a tense muscle in her neck or something. Shifting a little, she faced down the length of the bed, to where I thought my memory said there was a mirror. Her hands disappeared in front of her, like she was cupping her breasts or something. A little sigh escaped her, then, bending over, she slipped her drawers down around her ankles and stepped out of them.

She tried to do the whole "loop your foot through them and try to toss them in the air to save you from bending over" thing. Two failed attempts later, she just bent over and scooped them up. They went sailing through the air somewhere out of my line of sight, a laundry hamper, no doubt. And then she turned back to the closet and I saw her eyes for the first time.

So back in the day, one of my favorite movies was that old eighties version of *Dune*. I would get baked and watch it over and over. I mean, it wasn't exactly good, and it was pretty damn different from the book, but fuck me if I didn't like it. And part of that was that I loved seeing the blue-within-blue eyes, and how they sorta glowed.

Now this lady, her eyes weren't exactly like that, but there damn sure was a faint blue glow to them. Faint enough that I likely wouldn't have been able to see it had she been facing the light. But with the bulb behind her back-lighting her head, I could just barely see it. It was blue like deep water, but with a faint luminescence. It weren't natural, that's for sure.

She was looking up, overhead to a shelf. Reaching up, she started grabbing something. I coulda reached out and touched her with ease, that's how close we were. But she wasn't paying no attention, or she was half blind to not see me crouched there. There weren't that many damn clothes in the closet, and being eye level with her nethers like I was, all it would take was a little look down for her to see me.

Grabbing two towels from up above, she promptly closed the closet on me. An echo of seventies bush haunted my vision still, but I managed to keep it together. Listening close, I could hear her starting to leave, even over the beating of my heart. The little bit of light that was coming in flicked out as she left the room, the sound of the trailer creaking as she walked filling my ears. It was followed by more chatter, more laughing, and then eventually the opening and closing of a door.

Sure, I had known what I was doing was pretty fucking dumb, but it had seemed like a good enough idea at the time. Which, honestly, describes about 90 percent of my life. But it was exactly the kind of thing that would get my ass sent to jail, and after such a narrow brush with it . . . well, my heart was racing.

Sitting there in the dark for a bit, I worked on calming down first. That took a minute, but then I sorta wrangled with facing my own stupidity. Deciding that would take too long, I just listened for a few minutes to make sure that everyone had, in fact, left the house. It wouldn't do to try and slip out and just walk right into someone.

Once I was sure, I slowly slipped out of the closet. Stepping over to the bed, I chanced a quick peek out the window. The lights were still going, but everyone but the big woman was gone. And let's just say that big woman was showing off, well, *all* the goodies. I couldn't see them all that well, as she was mostly facing away from me in the chair she was sitting in, looking out over the water and clapping.

There were piles of clothes scattered about the place, and then it hit me.

Them old folks had gone skinny-dipping.

Jesus wept.

Some Things Can't Be Unseen

If all them old folks were in the water, it hit me that no one would be in the trailer they had been parked out back of for the past hour or so, which meant that maybe I could sneak inside and see what might be causing all this. Daryl had said something about a blue light, and that woman's eyes had been glowing blue. I'm a fool, but even I can add two and two and get four. Sometimes.

But my close call just a couple of minutes earlier had me a bit rattled. I was under no illusions; one bullshit arrest and I would probably lose Anna. I'd been on thin ice, and while we'd settled back into our usual level of comfort, she'd always made one thing clear to me. She didn't care what I did when it came to drugs—rather, she did care about the heavy stuff but just wasn't gonna fight that battle—but she wasn't gonna date someone in jail. I had to keep my shit together in that regard, or she would be gone.

Would she understand there were mitigating factors? That I had been asked to do all this by Lidda? Or would she hold to the letter of the law? I wasn't sure, and if I made it out of this night unscathed, I planned to try and get a little clarity on the matter when the time was right.

I decided to play it by ear. I needed to get out of this trailer, I knew that much. Once I was outside I could see what the lay of the land was, and then see if slipping in next door made sense. One thing at a time.

Slipping through the darkened house, I threw my beer can into the kitchen trash can. I decided to take a quick peek in the fridge and was delighted to find that a couple of beers remained. Liberating one from its chilly prison, I made my way over to the door that led out into the front yard. I took one last little look around, then cracked open the bottle and stepped out into the night.

Taking a few small sips of beer, I made my way over to the corner of the trailer. Taking a deep breath, I slowly, ever so fucking slowly, nudged a bit of my head around the edge so I could see out into the water. My one eye was able to take it all in, and what I saw . . . well, it wasn't great.

Them folks were all splashing around in the lake like a bunch of teens. Their pale flesh shone like fish meat under the light of the moon, and there was entirely too much of it on display for my liking. A few were swimming, so I could only see their head and maybe the occasional arm and shoulder, but most were in the water up to at least their waist. On the male side of things, I was mostly shocked by just how hairy they were—they looked like they had bits of white shag carpet glued haphazardly about their chests. On the females' side, well, what I was seeing was not Sunday school approved. One poor soul must've had breast cancer at some point, two thick lines of scarring sitting across her chest. The others, much like the lady I had seen up close and personal a few minutes earlier, well . . . let's say the years had hadn't been all that kind.

In a weird way, though, it would have been really sorta refreshing to see. All them folks, not caring what people thought, embracing their bodies for what they were? That was something pretty special, I reckoned, 'specially in this day and time. I might not have wanted to join in—ain't no one but Anna got a hankering to see my too-skinny, drug-ravaged carcass in the clothes God gave me—but folks having a good time, damn the consequences, was something I could get behind.

So yeah, it *would* have been refreshing to see, if every last damn one of them's eyes weren't glowing blue.

It set my skin to crawling, to be honest. There out beyond the light of the porch, they had naught but a bit of moonglow to illuminate them. In that darker space, the pale light of their eyes showed up in earnest. It was like a small swarm of paired lightning bugs, flickering with every turn of the head, every blink. I doubted I could have seen it from the tree line or the road, but close as I was, I could get a pretty decent look at it. This was not good.

Were they possessed? I hadn't ever heard of something possessing a group of folks, but you could fill a world of libraries with books detailing all the shit I didn't know about the supernatural. All I knew was that I didn't know what was at work here, which meant I had no idea how to stop it. I just knew that it needed stopping.

I mean, this was basically rape, right? Something compelling folks to fuck? Or was this more like a couple of beers getting someone a little loose and them doing what they didn't have the balls to do otherwise? I didn't know, but it was fucking icky.

Not as gross as the disturbingly pendulous set of balls on one of the guys that decided to grace my eyes with as he leapt into the air to make a large splash. Those nuts flapping in the wind as he went sailing into the water will probably haunt my nightmares for years to come.

But all in all, I had seen what I needed. Damn the potential consequences—I had to get into that house and see if I could find out what was behind this.

A Sumbitchin' Cat Burglar, Redux

With everyone at play in the water, I decided that I was gonna take a risk and just dash across the empty space between the two trailers. They were all caught up in some naked frolicking, and I knew that time was of the essence. Who knew how long they would be splashing around? I had to get while the gettin' was good.

That said, I did keep low to the ground and moved fast and smooth. The woman sittin' there with the oxygen tank was close enough to hear me if I made a ruckus, so I had to be a little careful. So, thinking quiet lizard thoughts, I slunk across the empty side yards from one trailer to the next.

With each house being sorta turned slightly compared to the next, it wasn't until I got on around to behind my goal trailer that I saw the pale blue light coming from some of the windows. I might would have thought it was a TV that had been left on, if not for the fact it was the exact same shade as those eerie glowing eyes. Worse, there were shadows in the mix, the kind that made it look like someone might be moving around in there.

I edged over and peered around the corner of the trailer. It took a minute, but I counted eight pairs of eyes bobbing around out there in the water, and the oxygen tank lady on shore, which made nine. That meant that everyone I had been watching was accounted for, leaving me to wonder who the hell was still inside. Was it another person, or whatever was causing all this shit?

If it was a person, there could be a short trip to a jail cell in my future. But if it was a creature of some sort, I didn't know if I was ready to handle that. Not a lot of wiggle room in a trailer that small if things started to go sideways. I thought about the snuffling thing that I had gotten a hint of when I used my magic, and the thought of facing that in a tight space was, uh, not appealing.

I wished I had some of my little golden shrooms. A couple of those, and I could get a much better grasp on what was going on beyond the veil, as it were. But my usual hookup for those hadn't been around in a while, and I'd had no luck finding some on my own. And I damn sure wasn't gonna go raiding Granny's grove to get some. I needed a grove of my own, I reckoned, but fuck me, you gotta have land for that—not live in a storage shed.

Just add that to the list of hurdles I needed to jump. But all that was a tomorrow problem, and first I had to make it to tomorrow, preferably without going to jail. So, I was just gonna have to play this more conventionally criminal and pray I didn't wind up in a cell.

That said, I damn sure wasn't gonna face it with my head on straight. Digging around in my pocket, I fished out a couple of pills. Had I been back at my shed, I'd have ground them up on this little mortar and pestle I stole from some store in the mall up in Montgomery about a decade ago. But, not having that, I had to make do with using my lighter and a little flat piece of metal I kept in my wallet for just such an occasion. Ain't a soul alive that would give me a credit card or such, so it fit just right in the spot where a bank card or such would have gone. Metal met pill met the butt of my lighter, and soon enough I had some powder. Up the nose it went, with the remnants left on the metal and lighter getting rubbed onto my gums.

It took a minute, but they hit quick, and like a ton of bricks. I was blanketed in this sorta thick, numb feeling. It was honestly too much, but I didn't intend on it staying in my system very long; I just needed a little bit extra just in case. If I got inside and all was good, I'd burn it off with some dumb magic before it had a chance to really fuck me up.

I made my way down the length of the trailer to the closest window that had the blue glow emanating from it. Getting close, I scooched up just close enough that I could sneak a quick look. And of course, it showed me a positively stunning view of a hallway. Of fucking course.

Turning my head left and right, I was able to figure out that whatever was making that glow was coming from a doorway I could just kinda see. Coming from a lifetime of living in and visiting folks who lived in trailers, I was pretty sure that doorway led to a bathroom. It had that look. Ain't a trailer I ever been in that had more than a tiny little bathroom window, always set too high for creepers to look in. So I knew that unless I wanted to go around to the side where everyone was hanging out and get a ladder, I was going to have to go inside to get to the bottom of this.

At least now I was even more certain it wasn't a TV.

I made my way back down the trailer until I got to the front door. Trying the handle, I found it was locked and swore inwardly. There was no deadbolt, though, so I was pretty sure I could handle this. Digging my wallet back out, I produced a much-used hotel room key and started using it to try and jimmy the lock. This wasn't my first rodeo, and this old key—which, if memory served, came from a night were Lidda and I had shacked up while hidin' from one of her many exes, ironically enough—had opened more doors than Carter had pills.

Sure enough, in less than a minute the door swung silently open.

Into the Belly of the Beast

Through the open doorway, I could see that there was a small lamp with a red bulb that had been left on in the living room, a tiny little thing that didn't do much more than make a shit ton of creepy-looking shadows all across the room. That, and show me a bunch of shit I'd never in my life dreamed I would see in person.

They had turned this place into some sort of geriatric sex dungeon. Either that, or some sort of kinky torture palace. Either way, as a red-blooded American male who was a teen when the internet came to Jubal County in earnest, I had seen most of this stuff before in porn. But in real life? Nope. It was, frankly, a lot to take in when you weren't expecting it. I ain't one to kink shame . . . but damn. They musta blown more than a couple social security checks decking this place out. The black of the leather with the red of the lamp sorta blended in with the shadows that cloaked the space around me, blanketing me in a cloak of blood-tinged daggers, ready to strike down the sins of the past, liberating me from—

Real it in, Marsh.

There were a couple of them big *X* thingies that you tie someone up to. A sex swing, too, though this one had a little stepladder beside it. I guess replaced hips couldn't climb in as easy. They had a bookcase that was slap full of paddles and whips and shit, made of enough leather to make a full-size cow hide. And then, lord, all the cushions. The floor had a ton of big-ass pillows and those, like . . . exercise blocks? I don't know what they're called, but they're like these mat things that look sorta like life-size Legos in a way? Firm enough to climb on, soft enough they won't hurt you to do it. I didn't even want to think about what they might be used for.

Gingerly, I stepped into the room, taking care to not trip over one of the many cushions. I was equally careful to not touch anything. The room was dark, the shadows were long, and my high was starting to come on real strong. I started to think I might be in trouble, knowing just what had probably touched every surface of this room, namely those tremendously droopy balls. Hanging low, swinging back and forth like a prodigious pendulum, clocklike in their fleshy horror, shocks of white hair making a bird's nest of—

Fuck.

I took a deep breath, trying not to think about how, in spite of knowing what had touched, well, probably everything, I kinda just wanted to curl up amongst the cushions and let the numbness and syrupy nature of all space and time wrap me in a warm embrace, dragging me down into its tender embrace as the vagaries of all history flowed in slow motion through my mind, revealing to me all the secrets I had ever cared to wonder about as visions of possible future realities curled inwards into the meaty, fleshy bits of my brain, cocooning me in a web of mystery and wonder as I went on a soft, pleasant journey within the depths of my soul and my psyche . . .

Fuck! Too high.

I was pretty sure my heart was slowing down. Or speeding up. Couldn't really tell. I was sure that it was getting real tight in there, which was never a good sign.

Without thinking, I called up my power—I had to burn at least some of this high. I couldn't think straight, so I did what felt natural, which was my newest spell. The one I had been practicing for months now. So practiced, I could do it in my sleep. I slurred the words out as clearly as I could, then twisted my fingers in arcane patterns from muscle memory, because I was too high to do anything else, much less think about if this was the spell I should have been casting.

My fists abruptly erupted into balls of black flames. They burned darkly, like flickering shadows tipped in hints of white-hot heat. They didn't harm me, and in fact they spread up my arms until I was sheathed in flame up to the elbow. At the same time, a circle not unlike a crown erupted on my head made of tall flames that looked, frankly, terrifying, at least to me.

I'd learned I had a gift for flames. Uncle HD said that most spellslingers had a specialty or two. Some like Granny might have three or four. I was pretty sure that hers were probably blood magic, controlling crows, memories, and spell jars. If those were things you could even specialize in . . . not like she was telling me shit.

But yeah, I had a thing for flames. This was the outgrowth of what I had been learning. Getting my little fireballs to turn into a stream was step one. Then, I reckoned I needed something maybe a little bit better designed for keeping shit off me. So, I came up with this, inspired by something I saw in a book HD had loaned me. It might not stop me from getting smacked, but it would make sure that if anyone tried to hit me, I could fuck them up right back.

I was tired of being knocked out and breaking bones, if I'm being real honest.

Some of the cushions by my feet started to curl and smoke a little as the heat of my spell—which, by its very nature, couldn't hurt me or anything I had on—got a bit too close. I wouldn't have noticed if I hadn't started getting a little less high, probably, so it showed that things were working as they should. My mind started to straighten itself out a bit, at least enough that I wasn't about to lose myself in the abyss of my own consciousness.

Don't get it twisted, I was still pretty high. But I didn't think it would kill me now, at least not before I got things hopefully straightened out here. So, with a flick of my wrist I killed the flames, though a hot sulfur smell lingered in the air. It wasn't nothing a little Febreze wouldn't fix, I figured, as I stomped out the corner of one particularly smoking pillow as it edged toward catching fire. After all, I was here to solve things, not run off a perfectly good tenant by burning down their house.

God, the mental image of how Lidda would react if I burned this place down was bone-chilling. I shuddered at the thought.

The combination of still being high and thinking about Lidda caused me to miss that eclectic feeling that had hit me the last time I used magic. But that spell had been a small thing, and limited to my hands. This time the feeling covered my whole body, and clear as day I got the vision that I was once again SEEN. More clearly this time, I got the impression of that seeking, blind, questing bird thing, a creature of the winds no man has ever laid eyes on. It was a haunted, hunting thing, and frankly it terrified me. Then it became less of a feeling and more a vision as it hovered into view there in the tiny trailer.

It found me there, as though it had sailed across some fathomless void, and began to circle me in a looping spiral. I could hear it snuffling through the jagged holes of what was like a madman's interpretation of a vulture's beak, breathing in my scent deeply as it neared. I was frozen in terror while, like a shark, it drew steadily closer as it pinpointed just where I was. Suddenly it darted toward me, its gaping maw wide and filled with craggy teeth.

So sudden was it that I didn't even have time to raise my arms defensively. I tried, but it just passed through me, a frigid wind that stole my breath away. I felt a huge chunk of my power drain away, as though it had feasted on my drug-fueled energy and stole it for its own. And then it was gone.

As it passed, after a far too long period of time, I was embarrassed to find I had pissed myself a little. Well . . . maybe more than a little.

I collapsed to the floor in relief onto the closest pillows without a care for just how laden in bodily fluids they might have been. As I slumped down, I saw that one of the pillows that had been behind me, out of my direct line of sight, had caught fire a little.

That's about right, I thought to myself as I fought off the urge to faint.

Magic Is Sexy

I'll admit, I was shook to the point that I didn't do what I should have and just jumped on putting out the fire. I mean, it wasn't that bad, but there was a whole lot of wood and faux leather in the area—all things that probably would have gone up in a blaze of glory if I gave it a chance. But the flames were small, and I needed a second.

In the end, it was the smell that motivated me more than the actual flames. Whatever that damn pillow was made of stank as it burned. *Bad.* Enough to set me to gagging, which got me moving with a quickness. I got to my feet and took to stomping on that cushion. And when that didn't get the job done, I used another larger pillow to help smother it. Of course that one caught a little of the flame in the process, but that fire, I was able to stomp out. So yeah. Crisis averted.

I debated trying to hide my handiwork, but I eventually decided against it. The fuck would it matter? Either they would show up while I was still here, in which case a couple burned pillows would be the least of my trouble, or I would be gone and they could just live with a little mystery. It would probably make for a great story.

Like the time I had found a half-eaten sandwich in my mini-fridge. To this day, I have no idea where it came from; it was just there one morning. Tasted good, too. But it's remained a little mystery that I think about from time to time, a fun story I can tell at parties. Really, I was doing them a favor by letting singed pillows lie.

Really, I was just thinking about anything I could to not think about that . . . thing. Whatever it was.

I decided that if I went to that bathroom and that creature was in there, I'd come back out here and light the pillows up on purpose and just burn this place down, damn the consequences. I wasn't gonna play that game.

Now that I had a moment of relative non-high peace, I looked across the living room into the kitchen and beyond into the little hallway. I could see the blue light there, sure as the world. It was bright enough that it flowed into the kitchen, where it met the red light of the lamp, making a muddy purple-tinged mess. It was coming out the door, just like I had seen, and I knew that was where I needed to head next.

I looked down at my wet crotch. I was a goddamn mess, but it wasn't like I had a change of clothes on hand. I mostly wanted to get out of the sodden boxers I had on, but the thought of them old folks coming in here to catch me bare-assed as I pulled them off was enough to make me decide to just ride it out. It sucked, but there wasn't anything to be done just then. And maybe I would stumble into a dresser that had some me-sized jorts in it as karmic payback for me agreeing, stupidly, to take on this good dead for no reward.

"Fuck it," I said, maybe a little too loud, but I was still scared as hell. My voice certainly sounded loud in the eerily quiet living room, which didn't help settle me down any. So, without a further word, I squared my shoulders and set out across the living room.

It was somewhat slow going, as pillows make a shit floor to walk on. I was having to take my time and step between them, but since there were so many, I ended up just kicking a path through them by sorta shuffling my feet along the carpet. It got a little easier when I reached the kitchen. I seriously considered checking the fridge, because I am not one to ever learn a lesson, I guess, but before I could, something caught my eye.

There, on the small kitchen table, next to a bowl of what looked like Rotel dip and an equally large bag of tortilla chips, was a book. But this was no ordinary book.

Its cover was leather-bound, or at least I hoped it was—like cow leather, not human. I really hoped. On the front was two folks doing the nasty doggy-style in an ornate sorta way. Like, it wasn't porn, exactly—it was more like what you'd see in them old Indian depictions of, like, the *Kama Sutra*. It wasn't exactly like that—it looked more Middle Eastern, I thought, than South Asian, but then I live in a storage shed in Alabama. The fuck do I know?

Swirling around these two people was some sorta cloud, like maybe, smoke? Only it sorta turned into a kinda human shape toward the top of the book cover, with its arms spread wide. It was just vague enough that it could have just been some weird smoky cloud, but there was a real feel to it.

It also looked old. Like, really old. It was hard to gauge exactly—the light was pretty weird in the kitchen between the blue and red light sources—but I had at least seen more than my fair share of old books. Mostly grimoires and spellbooks, mind you, which, the more I looked at this thing, the more I felt like that might be what we had here. Grimoires don't usually emit any sort of magic, but spend time around enough of them and you'll see they have a sort of feel to them. It's impossible to explain, but it's how I felt the very few times I had seen Granny's collection, or the books HD had tucked away. And that's how the couple I had felt.

I flipped up the cover and sure enough, it was a spell-book. A sex magic spellbook, if the pictures were any sort of indication. It had never occurred to me that such a thing might exist, but now that I saw it, of course it did. Anything mankind can come up with, if it can be tied to sex in any way, we're gonna figure out how. So of course there was such a thing as sex magic. But backwards-ass Jubal County, with its bizarrely puritanical false virtue signaling, naturally wouldn't have even a hint of such a thing.

The question was, Did someone here have actual magic ability, or had they managed some sort of fucked-up accidental summoning or such?

My answer lay in that bathroom. Begrudgingly, I set the book aside for the moment, though I fully intended for it to come home with me when this was all done. No, I had to get shit handled first, then I could make off with my prize.

The hallway was only about six or seven steps long total, and to get to the door only took half that. I strode up so I was right before the open doorway, just out of sight, and took a deep breath. I didn't have a whole lot of magic left after whatever that weird creature was stole a bunch, but I had enough to make things pop off if needed. So, with a roll of my shoulders, I turned the corner.

Was This Whole Story Just an Excuse for a Terrible Pun?

Despite the pale blue light roiling across the small room, it was surprisingly shadowed. Enough so that it took me a moment to piece together what I was seeing. And really, it was the sudden movement that caused everything to really come into focus.

The room was pretty tiny. There was a sink to my left and right beside it, a toilet. Not a real full-size one, mind you, but one more like what you would find in a camper. Then beyond that was a bathtub. Not a claw-foot or anything fancy—just your usual trailer tub-shower combo—only there was no longer any curtain on it, though a half dozen cracked plastic rings that had probably once held one remained.

That tub was the source of the light, but somehow it was also the most shadowy part of the whole room. This close, the glow pulsed lightly, leaving ripples like the reflection of an indoor pool on a wall at night. It rolled off a dark mass in the center of the tub, a blue-black shape that looked like a mix of smoke and stone.

Then a pair of eyes opened in the middle of that mass, and I realized I was staring at . . . well, I didn't know what the hell I was staring at. But it was alive, whatever it was.

The thing in the tub stretched and shifted. Turned out it had been hunched down, like it was squatting. Only as it rose could I see it didn't really have legs. Where its legs would have been, if it had been human, was a swirl of blue-tinted mist that gradually solidified into a thick waist. And fuck, was it tall. When it was done rising to its full height it towered over me, its head having to hunch over to not hit the ceiling.

Its chest looked like it had been roughly carved from a solid block of dark marble, black as soot and threaded through with large swooping spirals of blue. Its arms were heavily muscled, like something a comic book artist would draw on a superhero, and many of the spirals from the chest carried on down the length of the arms, swirls following the swell and flow of the bulging muscles.

Its head was the most human thing about it, save for the fact that where the eyes would have been were two orbs of fiery blue flame. It was totally bald, and there on its forehead was a single golden spiral that looked like it had been burned into the thing's flesh. The heat of it was still oozing out in a faint golden glow.

I was, truthfully, awestruck. I didn't know what it was, but it was beautiful and terrifying all at the same time. I might have stayed staring at it a long time, but then it lunged at me, its huge arms erupting into a cobalt blaze.

Calling up what power I could, knowing I would be too late, I went to cover my eyes as it collided with an invisible wall. White-hot sparks flew as it slammed its body into the barrier over and over, growling and snarling in impotent rage. That didn't mean it stopped me from ducking out of sight into the hallway, giving thanks I had already pissed myself . . . again.

When I was certain I was still alive, I peeked around the corner, slowly, and saw that it had spent itself against the invisible barrier. What do you say in a case like that? I hadn't a clue what I should say, so I just winged it. "You good there, killer?" I asked, keeping my body mostly in the hallway.

"Free me from this prison," it snarled. Its voice was like two stones being ground together.

"How 'bout we start with what the hell you are first." I needed more info, and preferably not from a bunch of nekkid old folks.

It crossed its arms and, I think, tried to look totally aloof. But when your eyes are fire and I just saw you lose your shit, that's a hard look to pull off. "I am a djinn."

Shit. I hadn't ever seen one before, but I had read about them a little in one of HD's books. They didn't give wishes, more's the pity, but they had magic and could be summoned. And while I hadn't ever heard of them making people fuck, for all I knew, that was all they did. The creatures of lore in an area tended to reflect the folks who lived in an area. Jubal County, like most of rural Alabama, ain't got much in the way of an Arabic community, which is where djinn usually come up out of.

So why the fuck was it here?

I would have asked, but something hit me then. This was a djinn. In a bathtub. "Holy shit, you're bathtub djinn!" I started to giggle uncontrollably as all the stress and terror of the past few hours tried to bleed outta me. It almost instantly became laughter. "Bath . . . tub . . . djinn . . . gin . . . bwahaha!"

If the creature out of myth and legend before me saw the humor in the situation, well, it didn't much care to show it, clearly. Which was its loss, 'cause that shit was funny.

I was literally crying, I was laughing so hard. I struggled not to lose my breath.

"Stop laughing, cretin, and free me from this prison!" It barked angrily when it finally had enough of my braying. That managed to reign me in a little bit, enough that I resigned myself to the odd chuckle.

"Sure, sure. Only I don't know how, and I don't know what the hell will happen when I do. For all I know, you'll kill my ass soon as I break you loose, if I even can."

"You have magic—I have tasted of it. Either give me enough that I can break myself free, or simply destroy this wretched tub."

"Breaking shit is my specialty. No sweat." I mean, I hadn't a clue how I would destroy the tub without wrecking the house beyond repair, but I could probably whip something up. That didn't address issue number two, though. "But I ain't doing shit until I know it's safe. You seem pretty fuckin' angry."

"I assure you, I have no desire to remain here even one moment longer. They have tainted me beyond all imagining—the pure light of my power has turned blue from all the pills they take. It will take centuries to cleanse myself, I imagine."

Blue pills. Viagra. I guess sex magic only can take you so far if the little soldier won't stand at attention. But how the fuck that had gotten mixed up with . . . you know what, I didn't want to think about it. Not even a little bit. But nothing he'd said was putting me at ease. "And you don't want to take revenge on them for that? Not even a little bit? Yeah, I don't buy it."

If I'd been turned a different color from someone else's drug use? You bet your ass I'd be hopping mad. If it was my own drug use, that was one thing. But someone else? Nope.

Finally, the big creature grinned. I wish it hadn't. "I have seen their minds. When I am free and they no longer draw on my influence, they will remember all that they have done, and the shame will be such that no punishment I could mete out would ever be as delicious. I have fed those lusts, broken down those walls, and planted that field into full ripeness over weeks now. This will be a harvest unlike any other I have had, and their wails of shame will nourish my soul for a thousand lifetimes."

"Savage," I commented.

"Indeed."

In the end, there were a few factors at play. First, that thing couldn't stay in the tub; it had to go, and sooner rather than later. I don't know how these morons had managed to summon it into a goddamn bathtub, but this couldn't continue. I'd told Lidda I would handle it, so I would handle it.

Second, let's be real. If that thing wanted to kill me, or anyone, I doubted that, long-term, there was anything I could realistically do without months of prep. And I didn't have months. And really, I didn't exactly hold my life in high esteem, if you catch my drift. I'm not saying I would've been better off dead, but Anna probably would've been without me in the picture. At least a little bit. And the guilt Lidda would feel would nourish *my* soul for a thousand afterlifetimes.

Most of all, though, I had pissy britches, and I wanted out of them. I was four pounds of "over this shit" in a two-pound sack. I was fucking overflowing with "over it." I just wished I had remembered to bring my magic cane pole . . . that hefty little shit would've made quick work of that tub.

Cracking my knuckles, I called up some flame. "Aight, then. Let's do this."

The Tale End of the Shaggy Dog

The moment the flames hit fiberglass, things started to pop off. The fire almost instantly took on a greenish cast, the tips of each flame burning white-hot. The tub caught quickly but burned slowly, far more slowly than I would have thought. It was like it was having to work extra hard to burn through the latent magic that had bound the djinn to the tub.

As the flames rose, it was like the shape of the djinn began to slough off and melt away. It was like that scene where the Nazi sees the Ark of the Covenant, and his face starts to melt. Blue skin began bubbling and churning as the heat hit it as though instead of flesh, it was made of candle wax.

Beneath that outer shell was the monster I had seen when I cast my magic. Only now it really was there in front of me, and if anything it was even more horrid. Strips of blue flesh hung from it like a rotting corpse left in the sun too long. Wings spread out from its back, filling all the space in the little room, wrapping around me like some sort of jet-black cocoon of shadow.

All light but the fire was obliterated within that void, and even that was dimmed dramatically. I stepped back, trying to get to safety without taking my eyes from the djinn, but I just bumped into those wings. Wherever they touched flesh, they set my skin to itching like fiberglass, as if instead of hair like a bat or something fuzzy, it was more like that on a spider's legs.

It's blind, snuffling head, which had been bumping against the ceiling, lowered toward me. Those empty orbs that echoed with just the faintest hint of blue-white light drew ever closer to me, and I found I couldn't look away. I was frozen, though by terror or magic, I couldn't tell. Not that it fucking mattered.

Its beaklike jaw parted and I could see those rows and rows of teeth, bits of rotting meat caught between them, getting ever closer to my head. Its breath smelled like sulfur and death caught on a hot western wind. I was pretty sure I was about to get chomped to fucking death.

Then it sighed, sending more of that sickly breath up my nose, causing me to gag. I saw then that where there had once been a floor there was now only endless void, a sinking abyss that I was floating over, some nameless, starless space from between the ends of the worlds. It was hit with a tremendous sense of vertigo, and suddenly I was throwing up. While I stayed suspended in the air, my puke vanished beneath me into that ever-growing ebony expanse.

And then suddenly the floor was back.

The djinn was as good as its word, and the moment I had burned away enough of the tub, it vanished. I'd say in a puff of smoke, but I think the smoke was coming from the burning tub, not the act of returning to whatever nightmare plane of existence critters like that called home. And since I was smarter than I looked—sometimes—I just turned on the shower and let it put out the melted bits of the charred tub. It was all real anticlimactic after thinking I was about to get eaten, just like I liked it.

It took me a second to get my bearings back. I could taste the thick taste of bile in my mouth, but there was no puke on the floor in front of me. Small blessings, I guess.

I heard some shrieking outside as I reckoned everyone sorta came to. A bunch of church folks suddenly finding themselves all wearing just a bit of murky lake water and moonlight? Well, my only regret was that I didn't get to see it. But I knew my time was short, so I struck a trot, scooped up the book of sex magic from the kitchen, and dashed out the front door.

With a little bit of luck, the folks who lived in Sex Dungeon Central would think that the djinn broke free, stole the book, pissed on their living room floor, and burned their cushions. 'Cause I'd made it this far without getting caught, and by damn, I wasn't planning on it anymore. I mean, other than that brief interlude on the other end of a shotgun. But hell, that didn't really count, right?

I hunched up next to the wall of the trailer once I got out the door and waited for the whooping and hollering to die down. I heard the door to the trailer slam shut on the other side and could hear the tread of running footsteps within that oversized tin can. Even still, I held still for another ten minutes or so, giving everyone enough time to get good and escaped back into their houses.

I wasn't sure how long it was gonna take Oxygen Tank to get dressed and then drag her ass home, but I decided to err on the side of caution. The end was in sight, and if I could manage to make it out without anyone else's rear ends being in my line of sight, I would call it a victory on all accounts. I'd seen way too many full moons that night.

Carefully, I slipped over to Daryl's house and tapped lightly on the door. I guessed correctly—he hadn't been asleep. Old folks don't sleep, not really. Least that was my impression, judging from Granny, who kept all manner of odd hours. All the better to skulk around, I reckon. Sure enough, I only had to tap a few times before he popped open the door.

He had a frown on his face. "I heard a ruckus. That you?"

"Let's just say you ain't gonna have to worry about any more sex parties any time soon. Unless you start them yourself, I 'spose."

The man snorted, making it clear what he thought of that. Then he gave a little nod. "I reckon that's good, then. Has been a bit quieter of a sudden. Now go on, get. Some of us got to get some sleep, now that there ain't no party roaring all damn night."

He started to close the door, then paused. He sniffed, hard, then looked down at my crotch. "Son, you done pissed yourself."

And with that, he shut the door in my face.

I stared at it for a good minute, an odd sort of mayhem playing through my mind. If my bladder hadn't been empty, I might woulda pissed on his door or something. Instead, I just walked off into the trees like the bigger man I am, making my way up toward Lidda's house.

Anna was up there, waitin' on me. Me, of all people.

Sometimes, you know, life ain't so bad.

At least until your piss-soaked pants start to chafe going up a hill.

Can't win 'em all.

NOSE TO THE GRINDSTONE

Being the Tenth Tale in the Redemption of Howard Marsh

Rainy Thursdays, Am I Right?

L ogic would dictate that you couldn't teach a possum to play fetch. But I had it in my mind that if that possum was a magical familiar that you could sorta control, then you could. I mean, it only stood to reason. But like so much in my life, things were not going to plan. Horace, my possum, seemed built to disappoint.

I'd found a dog toy on the side of the road the other day, and the portly li'l beast had taken right to it. About a foot long, and shaped kinda like a mutant raccoon, he'd taken to hauling it around with him any time he was lounging around my shed, happy as a clam.

It was roughly stick-shaped, so I figured it would be perfect to toss around and play fetch with. So, after a bit of wrestling to get it away from him, I rolled up the shed door and gave it a toss. I was damn sure he'd trundle after it and I would get a kick outta seeing his fat ass waddle across the gravel.

It was raining a bit, sure. But Horace loved rain, if his tendency to get all muddy and then roll over my bedding was any sort of indication. But the little bastard just looked at the now-distant raccoon thing, then back up at me, then back at the dog toy. And damned if he didn't shrug.

He *shrugged.* Possums don't even have shoulders, not like us, but fuck me if he didn't give the most noncommittal shrug I'd ever seen. Then he waddled back deeper into the shed and scrabbled up into my broken recliner, clearly of a mind to take a nap.

I stepped over and scooped Horace up with a grunt, and vowed for the millionth time that I was gonna put him on some sort of diet before I threw my back out hauling him around. Setting him down by the door, I pointed him in the direction of the toy and sorta mentally compelled him to go for it.

Now, mind you, I had been working with him on this. Having a familiar isn't an instant, instinctive deal—it takes some work. Work and me don't normally mesh, but this seemed important, so I had actually been making an effort on occasion. We couldn't talk, as such, but we could sorta share emotional states, and with some practice I had gotten to where I could not only store some of my magic in him but could also compel him to do simple tasks.

I closed my eyes and focused on that dog toy, envisioning him scooping it up in his mouth and bringing it back to me. It was the best way to get him to do things, I had learned. Visualize what you needed done, and he would do it.

I opened my eyes to see him trundling back toward the recliner. Throwing my hands up, I stepped out into the rain and walked the twenty or so steps to where I had tossed the toy. It was raining, but not hard, and it's not like I was getting soaked. The rain was pretty warm, and it felt good on my bare shoulders. I stood there a moment, letting it wash over me, sorta staring up into the black clouds overhead. It would come up a storm soon, I could tell, but for a moment it was pretty calm, with only hints of real distant thunder.

Horace's fuckery had me annoyed, but the rain was calming me down. I looked back to my shed and saw him already curled up in my chair, his eyes closed. He was probably faking it, too—he liked to fake being asleep to get outta things, which was probably the aspect of his personality I most respected. I don't know if that trait came naturally or if he learned it from me, but either way, I thought it sorta showed how we were of one mind.

Which gave me a thought.

I dropped the toy and walked back into my shed. I grabbed a vaguely clean-looking shirt from the pile of clothes by the foot of my couch and used it to dry my hands. Stepping to the back of the shed, which only took about three steps, mind you, I scooped up the half-eaten Pop-Tart I had been munching on last night and had mostly forgotten about. The ants hadn't found it yet, I was happy to see. Making a point of crinkling the wrapper, I stepped back over to open the roll-up door.

Looking back, I could see that Horace had opened one eye and was eyeing that Pop-Tart in all its blueberry glory. Horace loved a Pop-Tart. And though I knew he was fat as hell, and by no means needed a Pop-Tart chunk, I also knew he would be dumpster diving behind the Dairy Queen at some point in the day eating scraps, so what was the point?

This time I envisioned him getting the toy, bringing it to me, and then, once he placed it at my feet, me handing him a bite of Pop-Tart. By the time I had my eyes open, there he was waddling past my feet with a bewildering amount of haste. In a flash, he had scooped up the dog toy and made the turn to come racing back to me.

But then the headlights hit him, and he dropped the toy and veered away toward the dumpster. I could feel how startled he was through our connection, as well as his pang of loss at the thought of missing out on the Pop-Tart. Before I could even try to call him into the safety of the shed, though, he had scuttled under the fence that separated the Dairy Queen from the U-Store-It.

Looking to my right, I saw a gray truck with "Norris Land and Timber" painted on the side of the door. It pulled up to my shed, and inside I could see Earl Norris rolling down his window. We'd never met—we didn't run in the same circles, let's say—but I knew well enough who he was.

Through the now open window, he nodded to me. "Mr. Marsh. I'd appreciate a bit of your time, if you wouldn't mind taking a ride with me."

I eyed the man pretty hard. If I had to guess, I would put his age in the lower forties, though I'm no expert. He had that weathered look of someone who had spent a lot of time out working in the sun, so he could have been a rough thirty-five or a well-kept fifty, for all I knew. What hair he had was buzzed short, and he had a pair of nice sunglasses hanging around his neck. Pretty typical "I work for a livin'" attire for Jubal County.

The MAGA hat was a pretty shit accessory, I thought, but then I was the one wearing nothing but a pair of ragged cutoff jean shorts and the most stately mullet this side of the Mississippi. Not exactly the height of fashion, and also not exactly dressed to be going out and about on the town with a man I didn't know well. "Where would be going, if I was of a mind to join you?"

Earl flicked his wrist back and took a look at his watch. The man had money, and a lot of it—that much I knew. But that watch was just plain and basic, and it looked like it probably came from Walmart. Not worth stealing.

"Watch tells me it's a touch after noon. I'll spot you to some lunch at the Catfish House if you ain't eaten yet. Got a proposal for you, and it's my lunchtime. May as well pull double duty."

I shrugged. I was never one to pass up a free meal, and it had been years since I had been to the Catfish House. But all in all, I was pretty sure I wasn't gonna like what this was all about. Folks with "fuck you" money didn't tend to talk to me. They usually just talked *about* me, in the form of a police statement. So, whatever this man wanted . . . well, it was enough to put a body into a bit of worry.

But there was another, more important consideration causing me to reign in my general tendency to tell the man to fuck off and leave me out of whatever bullshit he had brewing. He might have "fuck you" money, but I had whatever the poverty version of that was in that it pretty much couldn't get any worse for me. But . . . he was kin to my girlfriend, Anna, and some of the kin she actually liked quite a lot. Ugh.

"Sure. Lemme grab a shirt and close up."

Friendly Chats

Once I got the roll-up door shut, I made a point to leave that bit of Pop-Tart as much out of the rain as I could where I thought Horace could find it later when he stopped being startled. Though, in truth, I was pretty sure he was eating his feelings in the dumpster just then, so I doubted he was too put out.

The rain was coming down a bit harder now, so I was fairly soaked by the time I got into the passenger seat of Earl's truck. It smelled of chainsaw grease and cigarette smoke, with an undercurrent of sweat. Typical work truck smells. The back of the cab was filled up with all sorts of tools and what looked to be a big ol' map case overflowing with topo maps. About what I expected.

Earl didn't waste any time pulling out back onto the road and heading us toward the Catfish House. He drove one-handed, and with practiced ease he set about tapping a smoke from a crumpled pack that had been sitting on his dash, then getting it lit. A little bit of rain came in when he cracked the window, but not enough to stop the man from enjoying his cigarette. He didn't offer me one, which I thought was mighty rude.

But it was a real awkward sort of silence, just the two of us sitting there in that truck and not really knowing each other. Normally I would have shown my ass a bit, said something to try and get a rise outta the man. Sort of set a tone, as I am wont to do. But . . .

Damn that woman. She'd sunk her hooks in me deep. *Deep* deep.

"So, you're dating Anna."

The tone he used was real factual, but with a faint undertone of . . . incredulity? Disgust? It was hard to read. He was clearly trying to be polite, as his Southern upbringing would dictate, but he was clearly not real hyped on the situation.

Or maybe I was just reading way too much into it.

"Gotta say, I'm not real pleased with that."

Well, maybe not.

I began slapping at my pants pockets and looking 'round all frantic-like. I could see Earl's face line with a bit of concern. "You missing something?"

"Jesus, yeah," I said with a sort of mock exasperation. "I guess I left all my fucks back at the shed, so I don't guess I can give one for your opinion on the matter."

The moment that man's jaw dropped, it gave me delicious joy like no other moment in my life, I think. It was like his whole brain was doing a cold reboot as he tried to wrap his mind around the fact that someone not only didn't give a damn about his opinion but was also willing to throw that fact right in his smug face. I was ready and waiting for him to explode in a fury, and I had some words all lined up to help me poke the bear. He'd gotten me a bit riled up.

But then he did something that surprised the shit outta me: He seemed to swallow his anger. Just gulped it down, and the red flush that had risen on his cheeks faded back to his normal tan. And then he gave a little nod, as though that was that.

"Fair enough. I suppose we understand each other. I'm not gonna apologize for wanting the best for my god-daughter, though, and whatever you think, I've never heard anything about you that would lead me to believe that you fit that description. Feel free to prove me wrong."

That sort of set me back, sucked the bluster right outta me, though I wasn't gonna let him know that. He had kindly struck a nerve there, as he brought up something that had certainly been eating at me the entire time we'd been together. Anna was great, and I was a piece of shit. She could do better, but I was damn sure not going to point that out to her. I knew a good thing when I had it, so I had been actually making an effort to try and not actively fuck that up.

"This why you treating me to lunch? So you can rile me up and feel better about how superior you are? Either way, I'm gonna eat that lunch; I just need to know how hard I need to tune out your talking so as I can enjoy myself."

Earl stayed quiet at that and just kept driving. The rain was really coming down, so he had slowed a bit. Even with the wipers going full blast, it was hard to see out the front glass, so I wasn't sure if he was being quiet because he was thinking or if he was just focused on not killing us. I was good with either, to be honest.

We were almost to the Catfish House before he spoke again. "You're important to Anna, so that makes you important to me. Important doesn't mean that I like you. It just means that I have a vested interest in you, if only to keep Anna from getting hurt. And that's all I am gonna say on the matter, unless you make me have to get back into it. But none of that is really why I'm taking you to lunch, at least not directly. It just had to be said."

"Fair enough. So why are we going lunch?"

"Because I have a job for you."

Fill Your Pockets with Lead and Silver

The Catfish House is an oddity. It's miles from any town of note without another building anywhere near it. And for a restaurant in Jubal County, it is large. My guess is that it was the biggest by a good chunk, but then I wasn't much of one for going out to eat. That would have cut into my drug money. Waffle House was about as fancy as I got.

This place wasn't fancy, though; it was just good old-fashioned Southern food. The place itself sat on a little bluff overlooking the river, squatted there like a frog about to jump in at any moment. I figured one day the river would shift and it would fall right in, but it had been open since before I was born and hadn't done so yet, so I figured it would be safe enough for lunch. Though the amount of rain coming down was enough to at least get you thinking about erosion.

Turning off the paved road, Earl guided the truck up the gravel drive of the restaurant. There were several dozen cars in the parking lot. The place was always busy, so we weren't able to get near the door and I made a bit of a scramble to the door in an effort to stay dry as possible. Earl wasn't having it, though. He just walked it, as though daring the weather to try and force him to do something in a way he didn't want to. I was pleased to see him duck a little, though, when lightning cracked across the sky a couple miles off. The man put on a good show, but he was just as human as the rest of us, no matter how hard he tried to act.

We were sat at the back in front of one of the large windows that lined the wall. Looking out, you could see the large patio area they had, though with the rain, no one was seated out there. But beyond that you could see the river gushing by, a brown snake threading its way past. It was a nice enough view for lunch, though I couldn't help but think about a certain giant catfish that I owed favors to. Just the thought of that resolved me to order catfish as a sort of petty revenge.

We had ordered and had taken our first sips of tea so sweet, I could feel my cavities getting worse before Earl decided it was time to talk turkey. I was so pleased at the thought of the forthcoming catfish platter I planned to devour that I even deigned to graciously listen to what he had to say.

"You know what I do, right? Norris Land and Timber, I mean?" he started.

"I've seen enough of your log trucks on the road, yeah. Cut timber, buy and sell land, that sorta shit. That sum it up?" Those log trucks were a menace, if you asked me. But then no one ever did, so why would you?

"That's the bulk of it, yeah. I have some other interests, but for the moment what matters is my timber business. It's been a bit cutthroat the past few years, but we've done alright." I suspected his definition of "alright" and mine were vastly different. "I have a bit of an edge in that I have a good rapport with a lot of the landowners in the county, so they tend to come to me first. So that's how I got this McGregor tract that's been giving me so much trouble, and that's where you come in."

My interest perked up at the mention of the McGregors. There had once been three major families with power in the county: the Marshes, the McGregors, and the Brennans. The Brennans were still around, but there was bad blood between our families, so they kept to themselves from what I had been learning recently. The McGregors though had once been close, but they had gotten dreams of more mortal power, and they chased them hard. Most folks had long forgot there had ever been whispers about them, as now everyone knew that they'd spawned a couple of state senators and even a governor over the years. The only Jubal County success story, near as I could figure, and of course they had moved away to Montgomery.

"Like out at the old McGregor home?" I asked.

He nodded. "The one and same. Not all of it, of course—that's a couple thousand acres. But they want me to cut about two hundred of it, good old-growth forest that's never seen a chainsaw, to pay for some kid going to college or something. It's over on the backside of the property, so they won't even know it's missing, little as they visit."

Everyone knew the Big House was going to rot, that the family had put Jubal County in the rearview and weren't coming back. I'm surprised they didn't have Norris cutting the whole property. Unless . . .

"So you're having some problems with it, and of a sort that made you think of me. I can run a chainsaw, but I 'spect you already got folks for that. So what do you need me for?"

Norris sucked his teeth. We'd come to the meat of things, and he was suddenly unsure of himself. I should have said something, sorta eased him into getting to things. But that would have made things easy, and I'd be damned if I was gonna make anything easy on this man. But then the waitress brought our plates, which bought the man enough time to settle on things, I guess. Once she had wandered off, he started cutting into both his chicken fried steak and the heart of our chat.

"Let me spell it all out for you, without you interrupting." He eyed me till I gave a little nod. I was focused on getting as much catfish in me as possible, as quickly as possible, in case he pissed me off to the point that I felt compelled to flip the table and storm out. Which I had even odds on happening.

"You're dating Anna, and I don't like it. But I know better than to try and run you off. That would probably just end up with you buried like a tick in her. So, I decided that I should work on you, try to help you become someone I would be happy for her to date, at least until she comes to her senses. I ain't a therapist or a drug person, but I got work that needs doing, and I know you aren't scared of work when it suits you. I've seen you coming out of chicken houses more than once, and that work is some rough work. So I just need to find work that suits you."

This was going to be good, I thought. I had to fight to keep from laughing, but thankfully the food helped with that.

"I also am not totally oblivious to the . . . stories about you, and your family. You've done a few things for people I know, and they vouch, if not for you, then for your ability in certain areas. I don't know how much I believe that kind of thing, but I believe it a little. Most folks seem to have forgot the rumors about the McGregors, but I sure enough haven't. And if I want to get to where I want to be, I think I may need a little of their type of mojo."

This was starting to get into dangerous territory, and the itch to laugh drained right out of me. "And just where do you think you want to be?" I asked, deadly serious for the first time since he'd picked me up.

He picked up his cell phone and tapped into his pictures, holding it up so I could see it. There was a picture of some guy holding a tiny infant. He was grinning mighty broad, and I could see a bit of family resemblance between the man in the picture and the man sitting across from me.

"That's my grandson. He's going to be governor when he grows up, either him or one of my other grandkids. And I am going to work like hell to get this family into the position to get him there, to earn the kind of money that buys legitimacy up in Montgomery. Like the McGregors. That's what I want. And if I need their kind of mojo to smooth the way, then I will get it, and I will use it. What I want is to know I have left a legacy that matters."

"I think you are trying to get the wrong Marsh on board with your plans."

His face soured. "You're talking about your granny. I've heard enough of her reputation that I would like to avoid her as much as possible. You're . . . rough around the edges. She's just plain dangerous."

He was right about that. I wouldn't get involved with Granny unless I had to; her gifts and favors all too often came due with a cost no sane person would want to pay. Norris might be an idiot for banking any money on me, but he wasn't wrong about her.

This man had me all sorts of confused. On the one hand, I was a pity project in need of rescuing. On the other I was, what, the court wizard helping blaze a path to future power? He needed setting straight.

"I've half a mind to just tell you to fuck off and finish my catfish in as much peace as you'll let me have. But I think you need a little clarity on things," I started. "The McGregors, without going into any sort of detail, had their shit together in a big way. Generations worth, all working in tune, plus a shit ton of money. Forty years ago, the Marshes, we might've had our shit together like that. Maybe, though we damn sure didn't have the money—I wasn't born yet, so I can't say for sure. But since then, things have pretty well gone to shit. And whatever you think I can do, I very likely can't. You want a full-blown wizard, but I ain't it. Least not yet, and possibly never."

It actually kinda hurt me to say that. Kinda brought to mind some long-buried thoughts about what might have been if my grandfather was still around proper-like. I think that's what sucked the fire outta me, and why I wasn't storming out of this place.

Well, that, and it was still raining fit to burst.

Norris nodded thoughtfully. "You wanted to know where I want to be. I told you. Either you can help make that happen, or you can't. Doesn't change things about Anna, though. So if you want it, I got a job for you the next week or so maybe. Depending on the weather."

He looked out the window as he said that, and I swear I saw his lip curl in disgust at the rain. I didn't know a whole lot about cutting timber, but I did know you couldn't run those big machines in the rain most times, lest they get bogged down.

He turned back to me. "This McGregor plot—someone has been sabotaging the work out there. Between that and the rain, we haven't got anything cut hardly, and time is money. I want you to be my night watchman out there, make sure no one messes with my equipment anymore. I'll pay you a hundred bucks a night, for as long as it takes, and as long as no more machinery gets damaged. You have a gun?"

I'll admit my eyes widened a bit at that. I'd had a gun once, but guns pawn real good. "No, not as such."

"I have a pistol you can borrow. We're a 'stand your ground' state. Anything happens, you can probably blast away and come out just fine in the eyes of the law."

I laughed. "I never come away fine in the eyes of the law, I can promise you that. Keep your pistol, I'll be alright. Just gimme a big ol' Maglite and a shit ton of batteries and I'll be straight."

I paused. When had I agreed to do this? I guess my brain had shut itself down at the thought of several hundred dollars coming my way just for staying awake. And I had just the perfect little cocktail to keep me up and going all night, no worries.

"Oh, and I need a cat carrier."

Fond Memories I'll Keep of Happy Ways

E arl had had things to do—work stuff, no doubt—so he left me back at my shed for a few hours to "catch a nap." I, of course, did no such thing. A normal person would have, sure. And with it still raining, it would have been prime napping time.

But instead I did a couple of rails, downed a few pills, then set about trying to lure Horace out of the dumpster without getting totally soaked in the process. My two-dollar poncho wasn't really doing a bang-up job in that regard, as you might imagine, so by the time I had the pudgy fuck back in my shed I was pretty damn wet.

The smell of wet dumpster possum is a heady blend of foulness.

I ended up just walking back out into the rain, since I couldn't get much more wet anyway, and took a pretty clean rag with a bit of dish soap and set to scrubbing Tubby Guts. I managed to ruin the rag, but by the time I was done he was substantially less sticky and smelled pretty tolerable. Horace, of course, acted as though he was Christ carrying the cross to Calvary and I was some Roman giving him the lash.

"He's a dramatic little bugger, isn't he?"

I glanced up from my work and saw Corey Davis, my neighbor, standing in the door of his roll-up dry as hell, and sipping a beer. I wanted that beer.

Beneath my hands, Horace was whimpering and rolling about as though it was coarse sandpaper and not a soft rag scrubbing him down. In truth, he was so fat, I wasn't entirely sure he hadn't just rolled onto his back and couldn't get back flipped back over. I really needed to put the bastard on a diet, or Anna was gonna kick my ass.

"Something like that. If I was Anna, though, he'd be acting like this was the best thing ever."

"To be fair . . ." Corey made a sort of hourglass motion with his hands. That beer just swayed there in my vision, calling to me.

But he had a point. I dare say anyone would rather have Anna rubbing them down than me. "Yeah, yeah. You gonna just stand there and give running commentary, or you gonna lend a hand by giving me a beer?"

So that's how I wound up trying to load a fat possum into a cat carrier, half drunk and all high, under the watchful, disapproving eye of Earl Norris.

But They Left Me in a Forgotten Place

Once Earl pulled out and got back on the dirt road that led away from the plot, I was left all alone in darkness. I clicked on my Maglite for a second, just to see how bright it was going to be now that the headlights of the truck were gone, then cut it back off. I was used to going about in the dark—that was how you got the best copper—so being without light didn't bother me a bit.

Earl had given me the grand tour, which took all of about a minute. There were two empty log trailers and two pieces of machinery that would be used to do the cutting and moving. That was it. They sat in a little clearing surrounded on all sides by either old-growth forest or the narrow strip of dirt road we'd used to reach it. The machinery loomed black in the darkness, lumps of darker shadow that were now under my diligent watch.

Well, and the trailers, too, but other than lettin' the air out the tires on those, there wasn't much you could do to hurt them. Least not without a hell of a lot of force. Or explosives. Thus, the focus was on the honkin'-big pieces of equipment, since they had lots of moving parts that could be messed up pretty easily.

I heard Horace rustling around in his cat carrier so, reaching down, I opened the door. He came waddling out, side-eyeing me pretty hard. He hadn't liked being carried in that; he was used to just riding in Anna's car loose if we ever went anywhere. But I hadn't wanted to take that risk in Earl's truck, and I doubted the man would have let me.

We couldn't talk as such, but I think I got my point across pretty well. He could see better at night than I could, though his vision overall wasn't all that great. But he did have one hell of a sharp nose, and that was sorta what I was counting on. I impressed upon him that if he smelled anyone sneaking around that wasn't me, he was to let me know. And if he did so, he would get a treat.

He trundled off into the dark then, his white-gray form disappearing into the gloom in a jiggle of plump possum fat rolls. I couldn't see him, but I could get a rough sense of where he was at all times. He had pretty quickly begun to start rooting around for some sort of grub or something to eat, but he was sticking close by, it seemed.

I decided to take a walk around the perimeter to help me get a feel for things. It was less that I was taking the job super seriously and more that I had a lot of drug-fueled energy that meant sitting still wasn't going to be possible for a good while. Walking around was just something to do.

I made my way over to the edge of the woods, walking carefully across the clearing. It was pretty clear this wasn't a natural clearing; this area had been carved out as a base of operations for Norris's people. As such, the ground was mostly churned mud interspersed with the odd stick or stump. The only part that wasn't a total mess was the little pathway that went from the dirt road on back into the depths of the woods. Clearly, at some point the McGregors had had a need to access this corner of the property, my guess being for hunting. But judging from the way the ruts had aged, it hadn't been used in many years.

Skirting the edge of the clearing, I was able to walk along this pathway for a good fifty yards. After that, the forest that had only been to my left started back on my right, marking the end of the open ground. I clicked on my flashlight, shining it down the path.

Forest lined the little road, barely wider than a good-sized truck. It curved away until I couldn't see it anymore, but near as I could tell, the ruts carried down its length. A few orange strips were tied to some of the trees, no doubt marking the edge of where to cut. Nothing else caught my eye, but I stood there for a few minutes nonetheless.

I felt . . . something. There was a heaviness to the air I couldn't explain, but I could tell that farther back in those woods, there was something outside the norm. I took a few steps forward and could feel that heavy sensation grow a little more palpable. It wasn't a terrible feeling, like something evil; instead, it just felt old. Like maybe the heaviness was the weight of years.

It may have been my imagination, or more likely the drugs coursing through my veins, but I swear that as I watched, the trees that lined that path grew closer and darker, and what little moonlight had shone through was blocked out by the overhanging branches threading closer together. Even the light of my Maglite seemed to grow more dim.

I stared, and watched, and eventually turned away and clicked off my light. I wanted no part of whatever was back there—of that, I was pretty sure. Thankfully, whatever it was, it wasn't my job.

It must have taken five or six walks around that clearing before I felt calmed down enough to try and ride out the rest of the night sitting down. Each time, I had paused at the edge of the woods when that feeling of heaviness had hit me, but as it never felt any different, I just got used to it and considered it the cost of doing business, as it were.

At some point I climbed up into the cab of some tree-chopping machine, banging my knee good and hard in the process. The string of curses lasted until I got settled into the seat and, clicking on my light—which I should have had on the whole time, I realize now—I saw that my knee was trickling blood now.

Rolling a fat joint, I reached out my senses to Horace. The little prick had found a perfectly sized mud hole for him to wallow in and he was there now, soaking it up. I know with every fiber of my being he did that just because I had given him a bath earlier. Spiteful bastard.

It began to rain, the soft patter of drops hitting the metal covering of the cab. There were no real walls or windows, so a few drops fell on my arm whenever the wind blew a bit harder. It was a warm rain, though, so I wasn't too upset by it. It wasn't blowing hard enough to put out my joint, so I just sat there in the quiet, basking in the green glow of the weed flowing through my mind as I stared out into the darkness.

With No Hands Around Bones

A round ten or so, I got off the phone with Anna. During the week she left me to my own devices, as she had to focus on nursing school, but she liked to end her day with calling me for some reason. So, I had gotten in the habit of keeping the worst of my depravity on hold until after she called. I told her all about my new job, and she seemed pretty happy with it. She went on and on for a bit about how nice it was of Earl to do all this—I left out the parts where he had called me trash. Wasn't no point in stirring up drama just then.

I'm not much of one for staying still very long—unless I've taken the right sorts of drugs, that is. I hadn't, though, so after two hours or so in that cab I was about fit to bust. It didn't help that on the way over, I had drank a good fifty ounces of soda and now had to piss like a racehorse.

As it was still raining, I was somewhat loath to go out in it. It had never really picked up, but it also had never really stopped. It was that kind of slow ground-soaking rain that was exactly what Earl didn't need. The ground was still going to be too wet for him to do his cutting tomorrow, though I didn't mind, as that just guaranteed an extra day of work for me.

Finally my bladder won out, and I climbed down from the machinery. I walked over to the edge of the clearing, where I hoped the trees would keep the worst off me, and handled my business. But by the time I was done, there wasn't really a dry spot left on me, so I decided I may as well have a bit of a walkabout. I could always dry off later.

It was a lot darker now, with the cloud cover blocking out the moon and stars, and I will admit it was starting to get to me a little. There may have been a touch of drug-induced paranoia as well, but only a touch. Pretty sure.

That's when I heard it.

I was on the far side of the clearing from the machinery, near to where the path disappeared back into the woods, idly strobing my light back and forth. The light did little more than cause some of the rain to show up a bit better, but it was still comforting to have in hand. But my comfort passed right quick as the cry reached my ears.

From deep within the woods came an eerie call. It was like the cry of a loon, but funneled through an old log. It rose in pitch toward the end before abruptly stopping with almost a popping noise. It cried out three times, like the world's most monstrous whippoorwill, the sound coming through the trees over the sound of rain and wind.

I couldn't recall having ever heard a sound like it, and fuck me if I ever wanted to hear it again. I felt a rush of fear coming off of Horace, and within moments I heard him crashing through the brush toward me. He damn near jumped into my arms, causing me to drop the Maglite. With my luck in full force, it hit the ground hard enough to shatter the bulb, and with a flicker, it went out.

Horace was a mass of quivering mud in my arms, and he buried his head into the crook of my armpit. He was making this snuffling, wheezing sound that was no doubt part fear and part exertion from running more than four consecutive steps. I myself was too freaked out to even start to worry about the condition of my shirt.

Was there a glint of bone out there in the woods? Was that shadow swaying out of step? Was that tree moving against the wind instead of with it? Or was the fear mixing with the drugs to freak me right the hell out?

Yes? Probably?

I bent over to grab the Maglite—even if it wouldn't work as a light, I could still club something with it. My refusal to take Earl's gun now felt very foolish, I had to admit. My back groaned as I straightened, Horace's weight putting on a good bit of strain on me. Carefully, slowly, I started backing away from the tree line, weighing my odds on trying to run when I knew no one lived for many miles from here.

That eerie call rang out once more. It was no closer, least not that I could tell, but that didn't mean it was any less freaky. It was long, low, and mournful now, with less of the urgency of its earlier, faster call. It still loosed three long cries, and as they sunk into me I could feel the sadness roiling off of it like a wave.

This time it was answered.

Coyote Grins

They started as little yips, like the barking of a small dog. But I knew that sound, and knew it well. Coyotes.

Soon enough the yips turned into howls, and through it all they steadily grew closer. I wasn't running, not exactly, but you could say I was moving with a sense of urgency. Coyotes aren't really something to be afraid of; they won't attack a human. Hell, you're lucky if you get to see one.

But firstly, they will, in fact, fuck a possum's world right up, and I wasn't letting Horace go down like that. And secondly, I had yet to meet a coyote that answered weird woodsy howling things, so I figured all bets were off at this point. I decided that playing it safe was the order of the day, and the safest place I could think of was back in the cab of that big machine.

By the time I had managed to climb up—which, mind you, was quite a feat with Horace tucked under one arm like the world's ugliest football—that yipping and howling had gotten pretty damn close. I peeled my possum off me and sat him down in the seat, and then grabbed my Maglite in two hands like a short club, ready for anything. I even started to pull up a hint of my power, just in case. I just tapped it lightly and felt a warmth start to flutter into my chest.

Pulling on my magic like that got Horace more fo-cused-like. He was still clearly terrified, and was trying to alternate between playing dead and scrunching up like he was going to jump back on me, but when a hint of magic hit the air, he sorta settled down. It was like he was getting ready, charging up in case I had to use him.

With no moon, no flashlight, and lots of rain, it may not come as much of a shock that there wasn't much I could see out there in the dark. I kept slowly turning around, because even though all the howling was coming from one direction, I wasn't gonna let something come sneaking up on me, not without a fight.

It was clear from the sounds of things that the coyotes had reached the edge of the clearing and were starting to come on in. It was impossible to tell how many there were between the rapid yips and the pounding of my blood. But it was clearly a goodly number, enough to make things real bad for me.

Suddenly, the yipping stopped. I froze, my eyes trying to cut through the gloom.

On the very edge of my vision, there stood a half dozen gray and tan coyotes. Their fur was matted down from the rain, but their ears were perked up, all eyes locked on me. They just stood there, not coming any closer but not sitting down either, looking like they could spring into action at any second.

A couple of them split off, and I lost sight of where they went. I loosed out a pretty nasty string of curse words, but low and mostly under my breath. At least I was pretty sure—terror had pretty well got me not thinking straight.

I kept trying to look around me, my head twisting like an owl, looking for the other two coyotes. But I was also keeping an eye on the four I could see in case they started trying to do something. I tried to impress upon Horace that he should be keeping an eye out as well, but he was in full-blown playing dead mode and wasn't really paying me no mind.

Not for the first time, I cursed that pudgy fuck.

Couldn't I have gotten a nice crow for a familiar? Nice and gothy, pretty smart? Maybe an owl, which would've been perfect for looking around in the dark right now? Nope. I got a very likely diabetic possum . . . who was equal parts loveable and useless.

Which, I mean, was kinda like me, but damn.

I caught a glimpse of movement to my left, and sure enough, one of the coyotes was circling around. I saw it for a few seconds before it became lost in the gloom once more. I guess it had been too much to ask for them to have just gone home.

That's when I heard a woman scream.

Ooo, Foxy Lady!

A shriek like you wouldn't believe came up behind me, like someone had just stabbed some woman about forty feet away. I shrieked right along with it, no doubt making someone think it was two women getting killed. Horace was gone—I had no idea where he'd gone off to, and I was way too out of sorts to even try and find out just then.

Instead, I did what I should have done from the first, but my drug- and fear-addled mind had forgotten. I sent a burst of power from betwixt my fingers, and with a couple of words I had an orb of brilliant white-gold light floating a dozen feet up in the air, peeling back the darkness in all directions.

Looking where the scream had come from, I saw a red fox with its mouth open wide. It loosed another of those shrieks, and I suddenly knew that it was no woman—just a fox. I was no stranger to fox cries, either, but even when I wasn't paranoid as all hell, they sounded just like a lady screaming.

But that was far from all I saw.

The clearing was packed full of wildlife.

I saw a trio of whitetail deer standing there, looking dead at me. In the trees that lined the clearing I saw countless birds, from smaller things like cardinals and sparrows to crows and even one fat barn owl. There were some rabbits, some squirrels, and a few huge wood rats. I saw a few raccoons, rubbing their greedy little paws together, as well as a few possums that clearly weren't Horace, as they weren't morbidly obese. Then those coyotes, of course—of which there were closer to a dozen, I saw now—ringing me in a circle. And every fucking one of them was staring dead at me.

And not a one was moving.

It was, I think, the most eerie sight I had ever seen, and I damn near dropped the Maglite as I froze. Any other time, those coyotes would have been partaking in a woodland creature buffet, but there the mortal enemies all just sat around each other, their beady little eyes burrowing into me. I was suddenly really glad I had just taken a leak, or I'd have wet my already soaked pants.

Over the sound of my own frantic breathing, I could hear Horace wheezing away. From the sounds of things, he had somehow managed to get under the seat, and I was certain I was gonna play hell getting him out from there. But then I almost laughed at my optimism that I would be alive to encounter that problem.

I wanted to crawl out onto the hood and from there get up on the roof. I thought I might be a little safer up there, at least from animal teeth. I was probably lightning bait up there, but at least that would be a quick death as opposed to being nibbled at and pecked to death by scores of nature's finest.

Horace was the problem. I wasn't going to just leave him behind. So, I crouched down a little and with one hand started trying to fumble around under the seat for him.

Ever drop your car keys or cell phone down the crack of the car seat and then try and get it out? Imagine that, but instead of nice dry car keys, it's a wet portly possum who is actively fighting against you. I'd have been better off trying to mud wrestle a hippo. It was quickly becoming clear that this was a two-hand task, and I loved Horace, but not in a "drop the only defense you got" kinda way.

Above me, my light was getting a little dimmer as I lost focus. When it did, I saw some of those critters start to nudge forward a bit. I stopped messing with Horace and sent a steadier stream of power to fuel my orb. As it brightened, the creatures recoiled ever so slightly.

It occurred to me that playing defense was probably just going to get me eaten.

I took a few deep breaths and worked to calm myself down a bit. My heart was still racing, of course, but I was able to calm my mind and start thinking a little more clearly. It was pretty obvious that there was some sort of magic at work here, and magic was what I did. Poorly, but still.

Sending my senses out, I began to try and get a sense of the magic at play. It was real passive-feeling, like a really weak version of what I usually took some magic mushrooms to unlock. Though, to be fair, I hadn't been able to do even that much a year ago, so at least I was making some progress. In my mind's eye it looked like green root-like threads that connected each animal to those around it. There were other threads as well that looked as though they were trying to wend their way toward me, but they were being kept at bay from the bright light of my orb.

Krista had been coaching me a little lately, and the main thing she'd tried to impart to me was that magic had tons of rules and patterns, sure, but a lot of it was just plain doing what felt right. And all those roots, they felt like some sort of night-blooming flower to me and my orb was the sun, ready to scorch them clean off this planet.

I tapped into Horace, drawing up the bulk of the power I had stored within him. I felt a huge amount of power start to flow into me, far more I could handle. But I had no intention of holding that power; instead, I just funneled it right into my light.

Above my head, my magical orb began to grow and pulse. I couldn't see it directly, what with the roof of the cab blocking my view, but I could see the result. All around me it grew steadily more and more illuminated, and within seconds it was bright as day within the confines of that clearing. It had some heat to it, too, and I could see little tufts of steam start to rise up from the ground nearest to me.

All those roots began to curl and burn, like leaves too close to fire. The stronger my light flared, the more they retreated. I saw them . . . unpluck, for lack of a better word, from each of those critters. Those threads that had been reaching out to me went up first, then those of the animals closest to me. As the roots detached from each animal, they looked around wildly, then bolted and ran.

As the glow expanded, more roots wilted and died and more animals were freed. Soon, the clearing was a chaotic swarm of animals fleeing in all directions, shrieking, howling, squawking, and chittering madly as they returned to the woods. I saw a coyote scoop up a wood rat as it fled and an owl snag something wiggly as it flew away.

Whatever truce the magic had created among the beasts was clearly over now.

In less than a minute, it was just me and Horace left. You had best believe I kept that orb going as long as I was able. Some folks might have saved a little power for a rainy day, but I figured it was already raining, and I was gonna scorch the earth of every magic root possible until I was on the verge of passing out.

When the last sputtering bits of light finally ended, we were left alone in the dark. I really wished my Maglite would work, but that not being the case, I took this time to finally peel my possum pal out from under that seat. He'd stopped shaking, but I could still feel echoes of lingering fear coming off of him. So, I scooped him up into my arms, got us curled up into the seat of that big machine, and then settled down to wait for the dawn.

Forgive Me, I'm in Morning

Dawn broke slowly, and without much fanfare. The rain had stopped perhaps an hour earlier, but the clouds were still fat and gray overhead. It caused everything to look real muted, and with the thick surrounding of trees, what little light there was to be had barely made it to me. I didn't mind, though. Any light was better than the creepy gloom I had just spent the last few hours suffering through.

The rest of the night had passed uneventfully, thankfully, other than one or two claps of lightning that almost threatened to wake up Horace from the deep slumber he'd managed to settle into. It had gotten a bit chilly, and I'm not gonna lie, having him curled up in my lap made for a sort of bootleg heater. The dried mud on him had spiked his hair up into some rather wild patterns, I saw, and I groaned inwardly at the thought of trying to get him clean once again. It was a small enough price to pay, though, I supposed. All in all it felt really good to be alive, all things considered—a very, very rare feeling for me. Near-death experiences will do that for you, I reckon.

Norris rolled into the clearing a little after seven. He stepped out and when his boots sunk into the mud, he swore under his breath. I heard it, though I opted not to make note of it. Instead I just sat there, watching. He came slogging over after a few seconds of glancing around, no doubt doing a mental count of the high-dollar equipment and making sure it was all still there.

"Well, everything looks alright," Norris announced, a cup of Hardee's coffee in his hand. No doubt there had been a biscuit paired with that, and the grumble in my stomach made it clear to me just how good that would have been in that moment. I didn't see Norris as the thoughtful type; no doubt he believed that I should pull my biscuit up by the bootstraps or some such bullshit.

"Yep," I drawled from my perch. I made no move to get down just yet. I figured I would let Norris have a look around while I began stretching my legs a bit.

"Anything happen last night?" he asked as he stared at the ground. No doubt he was seeing the remains of a number of paw prints, though the rain had likely obscured most of them. What he could see was probably a confusing mess that left more questions than answers. I wasn't in a particularly obliging mood.

"Nothing I couldn't handle. Don't worry, you got your money's worth," I said, scooping up Horace from my lap and setting him on the floorboard of the machine. That managed to wake him up, and he began to yawn and stretch. I followed suit.

Norris just nodded and proceeded to walk around the clearing, taking a closer look at each of the pieces of big machinery. After a couple of minutes, he wandered back over. "I reckon so."

He pulled out a well-worn wallet about as thick as a brick with credit and business cards. Thumbing into it, he pulled out a small stack of twenties, counted them out, and slipped two back inside the folds of leather, then passed the other five to me. "Cash in hand, at the end of every shift. A hundred, as agreed."

I took them and shoved them in my pocket, then wandered over to gather up the cat carrier for Horace. Behind me, Norris kept talking.

"Still too wet, though I think it's gonna dry out this weekend, if the weather man ain't lying to us. So it should be good to start on Monday, I hope. You're still good to watch through the weekend?"

I really didn't want to . . . but I did want that sweet, sweet cash. Weekend nights were also my prime time with Anna, and I would hate to miss those. But damn . . . three more nights, at least, would be four hundred total.

That was a *lot* of drugs. Hell, I could even catch up on some back rent. Maybe buy—

The image of all those critters staring at me with those hungry eyes flashed into my mind.

I knew I was gonna need a bit of help if I was gonna get this done, and it needed to be help I didn't have to pay for, or else what was even the point? My thoughts strayed to my family.

I looked back at Norris. "Yeah. I'm good for it."

And the Weekends Come and Go Like Tides

"Good, he stinks! For the last fucking time, can you please get him away from me?"

Krista was trying to shove Horace away with her foot, and not having much luck. Horace had a bit of a crush on my cousin, it seemed like, 'cause he'd been hovering underfoot for about the entire time we'd been there.

"There" being the clearing I'd spent the night in, of course, and "we" being Horace, Krista, and her dad—my uncle, Hubert Dale. It was a veritable swamp of Marshes, or whatever a collective noun of our branch of white trash should be called. A clusterfuck of Marshes? A debacle of Marshes?

Whatever the English majors of the world would call us, we were there in force to get me out of the predicament I had found myself in. It was clear that back in those woods was some sort of power that had its eyes turned on this cutting operation, and I had wound up being the single line of defense. And as I did not want said power to make me *actually* act as a line of defense, I had brought the gang out to help me throw up some wards.

That was the plan, at least. The execution was proving to be slightly more complex than I had envisioned when I'd had Norris drop me off at my uncle's.

HD had been waiting on me, of course; he'd known I was coming likely before I'd even known it. He dug out a book or two while I made myself some coffee and smoked a joint on the porch. Explaining to him what all had happened, well, it just sounded more and more like I had gotten myself into something real stupid.

HD thought it might be best to go talk to Granny. I vetoed that pretty hard and heavy. I was about to the point that anything having to do with that old witch, I wanted no part of. And she'd always been real squirrelly about the MacGregors, so I was dead set on not mentioning this to her at all. There was no telling how she might react, but however she did, I had no doubt that I would get fucked over somehow.

In the end, we compromised by calling up Krista, who had predictably been a little pissed to be dragged into this. But it's not like she had anything better to do—she was the least busy hair stylist in the county. I said I would buy her lunch, fully intending to have HD do so when the time came.

And now we were here, walking along the edge of the clearing, making little carvings into the trees. My job was to make the carvings. I had actually been doing a little bit of practice when it came to making glyphs, which, I'll admit, was a bit out of character for me. But it was paying off now, even though I usually practiced with paper and pencil, not carving into pine bark.

But HD, who had made it his job to inspect each glyph, was there to have me fix the worst offenses, and then Krista would walk along behind and give it a little spark with her power. I was plum tapped out after last night, and Horace was empty as well. Making these little babies come to life required a bit more than I could muster without diving in pretty heavily into my drugs . . . which then would've made carving these glyphs real tricky. A vicious cycle.

It should have been a smooth, easy process: carve, inspect, spark, repeat. What actually happened was more like carve, inspect, fix, inspect, fix, argue, shout, inspect, curse, shoo Horace, spark, repeat.

In a perfect world, we'd have been done in an hour. But this was Jubal County, which is as far from a perfect world as you can manage, so two and a half hours later we were finally beginning to wrap things up. Really, I just needed Horace to stop trying to hump Krista's leg long enough for her to spark up the last glyph and things should be all hunky-dory.

I scooped up Horace and gave him a little toss toward the van, sending a strong impulse for him to leave us be a minute. It was even odds that he would listen, but my attention had already shifted back to Krista.

She was muttering a few words under her breath, and her hand began to glow with a faint blue light. Reaching forward, her finger came to rest on the bottommost line of the glyph, causing it to pulse. Blue light threaded up the lines of the carving until the entire sigil glowed. A moment later the whole thing pulsed, then went dark as she pulled her hand away. She was rubbing her hand a bit as if it was sore, which it might well have been; she'd cast more magic that morning than I could manage, by a long ways. Well, more than I could manage without drugs. Pump enough drugs in, and well, I could have that whole place glowing, I reckoned. Still, I would be lying if I wasn't jealous of just how much magic she had at her disposal. Granny had trained her well, even if it had been against her will.

I was not about to let on that I was jealous, however. Never. I'd rather eat my own tongue than admit something like that to my cousin. We had waaaaay too old of a friendly rivalry to let something like that happen.

"Well, are we done handling your light weight?" Krista asked, looking from HD to me. She opened her mouth to say something else snarky, but by then Horace was scrabbling at her ankle again. "Horace!" she roared as the randy possum proceeded to make tender love to her New Balance.

Moon Is on the March

A three-hour nap was not enough after that, not by a long shot. Norris had been pounding on my shed door far too early, if you asked me, which clearly he had not. I was a level of grumpy I was not really ready for, having pretty well come down off everything, getting woken up to a yelling old dude, and not even getting a chance to scratch my various itches before he had me herded onto the road.

I pouted hard in Norris's direction, but he ignored me. He'd been ignoring me since I'd insisted on bringing a certain cane pole along with me, even though there was no place to fish.

Really, what had me most riled . . .

Well, of course, it was the lack of drugs in my system.

But what had me *second* most riled was missing out on my time with Anna. It was Friday night, damn it! I should have been hanging out with her, getting into some shenanigans. Or her pants. Or in-her-pants shenanigans.

Instead, I was on my way to once again go sit in the dark. I had forgotten to fix or replace my flashlight, I realized, and it was too late to do anything about it. I hadn't even bothered trying to bring Horace this time, since I hadn't had any time to fill him up with power. No point in risking the little idiot, even if I thought it was going to be a safer night.

Well, it was more that I hoped it would. I didn't have any sort of sure knowledge, but I was due a bit of luck, maybe.

All too soon I was back, alone, in the dark of the clearing, watching the headlights of Norris's truck disappear down the road. At least it wasn't raining this time, but that was countered by the utter lack of light. I could have used my phone, but I needed to save the battery as much as possible just in case I had to call for help or something. I figured Anna would like as not call in an hour or two, and I wanted to have enough of a charge to last till my minutes ran out.

There was a little bit of moonlight filtering down, but it was intermittent, being covered by clouds more than not. They weren't the thick rain clouds we'd been having, but even thin and wispy as they were they still covered that moon right up, dimming the little bit of light there was.

It bathed everything in the faintest of silvery grays. All around me the machinery loomed, squat masses in shadow. Their edges held the light ever so lightly, lining their bulky shapes and giving them form. Beyond them the trees made a dark wall, impenetrable to my eyes, a jail cell made of tall pine.

I sent out a faint flicker of my power, a tiny speck, and surrounding me in a large circle, the glyphs pulsed purple. They faded instantly but left a fluorescent shadow on my retinas, almost two dozen chest-high swirls of color curling their way into the bark of the trees.

We had less than an idea of what might be out there. When dealing with powers beyond your ken, I had always found the best strategy was not a strong defense or offense, but to remain unnoticed as much as possible.

The MacGregors were an old family, and undeniably more powerful than mine. Whatever was out there, it likely wouldn't be good. Logic would dictate that it was unlikely they had left anything too, too powerful behind when they left our little county in their rearview mirrors, but you never know. There was every chance in the world they had left back some nasty little trap for Granny, knowing how she was like as not to come prowling eventually.

So HD had gone digging in his books and found a glyph that was just perfect. When folks sent out power in that direction, it would just sorta . . . slide off and around. Like water flowing around a rock in a river, was how Hubert Dale explained it to me.

It wouldn't work against direct action. So if whatever was out there decided to hurl some bolt of power at me, well, I was proper fucked then. But if it pulled another stunt like last night, sending a flow of power out to manipulate a bunch of critters, then they should sort of just flow around me. That was the theory, anyway. What was far more certain was that it wouldn't be able to send any sort of magical sensing into this clearing. Anytime it tried to scry me, its eye should just sorta glance over me. We'd put up so many because this sort of glyph worked well in numbers, which I had been unaware was even a possibility until we'd started.

I was going to paint the fuck out of my shed walls with this thing once I stole some paint and had some free time.

Anyway, the dream was that whatever lurked in the deep woods wouldn't be able to really see the clearing and would just leave it the fuck alone. And, more importantly, me.

There was just no way to test it, though. I wouldn't know if they worked or not unless shit suddenly got real bad for me. Which had me nervous, to say the least.

I skirted the edge of the glyphs, peering out into the dark forest, trying to see if there was anything lurking about. With all that tree cover and the moon being spotty at best already, it was wasted effort. I didn't see any movement, which was really all I could hope for, and the only thing I heard was the distant hoot of an owl. Just normal woods shit. Crickets chirping and all that. Normal.

I was weighing a nap. I mean, I wouldn't know things were sideways until they were actually sideways anyway. And that strange howling call that I'd heard the night before would probably wake me up, I figured . . . probably.

Or I could do a few bumps, maybe hit the pipe a bit. That would keep me up just fine, and charge me up in case the shit hit the fan.

But I was . . . tired. And more than just sleepy, if that makes sense. Tired to my soul.

I wanted Anna.

So instead of doing anything I should have or could have done, I just settled onto the tire of one of the log trailers and had myself a pout. And damned if it didn't start sprinkling just a bit.

Kill the Headlights and Put It in Neutral

I must have sat there about an hour, if I had to guess. Long enough for my butt to get numb and a little sore, so once I had worked out a bit of my pity party, I got back on my feet, gave my nose a good blow into my farmer's handkerchief, and started going on another little walkabout. It was more to stretch my legs and clear my head than anything resembling guard duty.

A flicker of light caught the corner of my eye. Turning back in the direction of the road, I saw a pair of headlights coming down the road. With all the trees between me and the car, they were almost like a strobe light, as the lights were constantly being covered by intervening trees. As it neared, I began to hear the steady thrum of its engine.

It suddenly occurred to me that I had perhaps been very foolish.

Norris had, of course, talked about some of the things that had been happening. And I had just linked it all with the MacGregors, and being me, my head instantly went to spooky shit. Last night's events only confirmed matters in my mind.

But that didn't mean that there might not also be some sort of eco-nut coming out here at night and messing stuff up. Hell, maybe what happened last night *was* some sort of eco-druid-wackadoodle getting up to some bull mess, trying to scare me off. And maybe now they were coming back to finish the job, only with a gun or something. There could be a whole carload of them, just raring to stick it to the rapists of old mother earth.

There was nothing, literally nothing, down this dirt road. It didn't even connect two places. It was basically just a little dirt track that outlined the MacGregor holdings, no doubt so they could get places that needed getting. There was no reason for anyone to be on this road, especially at this time of night, 'less they were coming to my clearing.

I looked around for something, anything, I could use as a weapon. I had my magic, of course, but that was a little on the low side. I could try and hit a quick bump to juice it up a bit, but that vehicle was getting real fucking close. I'll admit, I was panicking a bit.

Then I remembered my cane pole, which I'd left leaning over by where I'd spent the previous night. Moving quickly, I went and grabbed it, then hid behind the biggest of the machines. I kept my head sorta peeked around the corner of it, ready to get the jump on whoever it was if I could. I didn't call up my power in case my theory about some eco-druid was right. I wanted them thinking I wasn't there until I smacked sheer hell out of them with a magical cane pole.

Sure enough, the vehicle slowed as it reached the entrance to the clearing. I could barely make out that it was a car as it turned in. I ducked back behind the machine, trying to be careful lest the headlights pass over me. I heard the pop of tires crossing over bits of limb and log as it came on. Light filled the clearing from two bright beams, and I could see the long shadows they threw up.

It was close when I heard it come to a stop. I could faintly hear some sort of music playing loud and heavy, but the engine was mostly covering it. Then the driver killed the engine, and all I could hear was the ticking sound of the engine cooling down and, more clearly, the dulcet tones of some really brutal black metal. Dimmu Borgir I thought, though it was kinda hard to tell. But then the door opened, and I could hear "Progenies of the Great Apocalypse" clear as a bell.

My heart leapt.

I would have ran straight out from behind that machine, but I did have a reputation to uphold. As it was, I would describe my motion as a sort of sedate, regal scurry. There was a definite spring in my step as Anna's Ford Focus suddenly came into, well . . . focus.

"What the hell—?" I started, a smile splitting my face.

Anna held up sixer of Natty Daddys, returning my smile. "Fridays are our day, Marsh. You didn't think I was going to let you sit out here in the dark by yourself, did you?"

Using her free hand, she reached out and grabbed my pants, pulling me close. Then she leaned down to kiss me.

That woman. Damn.

It hadn't stopped drizzling, so we made our way back into her car, where we would be out of the rain. She turned the volume down to a level that would let us talk, though not too quiet, mind you. Anna had a real thing for music in general, heavy metal in particular, and didn't let much come between her and it.

I dug out a joint and we took to sharing it back and forth while sipping those Natty Daddys. She set out to tell me all about her week, and I just tuned in and let the green glow of weed and beer take the edge off me. I was happy.

Drugs didn't make me happy. They filled a void and scratched an itch, but that wasn't happiness; that was survival. Until Anna had come along, I couldn't remember the last time I had been well and truly *happy*. She made me happy in a way I hadn't been since before I got bad, and it was . . . almost painful in a way. It hurt down deep that I had been down so long. So many years of my life just consumed by the cycle of finding drugs, taking drugs, doing shitty things to find more drugs, rinse and repeat. My soul became so numb, it had forgotten how to be happy, or so I thought.

She could sit there and talk on and on about her day, and even though I knew none of the people involved or what have you, I hung on her every word. Just being around her made the bullshit fade for a bit, and when you're someone like me, that's worth more than all the gold in Fort Knox.

It made me think of Jerm and how, if he could've found someone like Anna, too, then maybe he would be alive today.

So all in all, it made me happy for her to be there. But selfish as I am, I was loathe for her to be up in my business on this night in particular. There was fuckery afoot, and I didn't want to risk her getting caught up in it.

That said . . . I knew if she left too soon, she'd like as not take those Nattys home with her. And, well, we couldn't have that. A Natty Daddy is a big beer—I wouldn't want her to strain herself, now would I?

As we sat there talking, the drizzle turned into a bit of a solid comedown, fat drops showing up in the view of the headlights and pummeling the windows. I knew that was going to play hell with them trying to cut this property, but I was here to stop hoodlums, not storms. I was no weather witch anyway; I didn't have the first clue about how to go about it. Granny, though . . . she could dry this place right out if she had a mind to.

Thinking of her kinda killed my buzz a little. So, I doubled up my drinking to compensate. I ended up drinking three beers to Anna's one and a half, and not gonna lie, they had me in a good place. We had a bit of a hot box going, too, what with the windows up. All in all, it was good stuff.

Finally, though, my greed was finally smothered down by my love, and I turned to Anna. "It might not be all that safe for you to be out here. Not really. So maybe you should head on home for the night."

She bristled a bit at that. "You don't want me here?"

I rolled my eyes at that. "You know that's not the case. I just don't want you getting caught up in whatever's going on out here."

That got her narrowing her eyes. "What do you mean? I thought you were just being the night watchman."

"You're right. It's just what I'm night-watching against might not be . . ." I sort of waved my hand around, fumbling for my words. I might have wound up a bit drunker than I'd thought, or maybe the lack of sleep was actually catching up with me. I resolved to remedy that soon as Anna left.

"Words, Marsh."

That jarred the words loose, so they came out in a tumble. "Normal? Human? Fuck, it's spook shit. You know. Hoodoo, dented cars, that sort of mess."

"Dented car" got her. You let one pissed-off giant satyr slam into her car, and boy, does she never let you forget it. She turned her head, looking out into the rain and, of course, seeing nothing. When she turned back, I thought I could see a little glint of fear, which made me sorta sad.

"So you want me to just leave you out here by yourself with some sort of magic crap going on? I don't think so. Plus, it's raining cats and dogs out there—are you just going to sit in the rain in the dark?"

"More like raining foxes and coyotes," I muttered. I pointed in the direction of the cab I rode last night out in. You could almost see it on the very edge of the headlights' glow, looming like some old ship coming out of the fog. "Look. I did just fine last night sitting in the cab of that big thing over there, and I'll be fine there again tonight. I mean, it's not like you were gonna stay out here all night, were you?"

She gave a little shake of her head, but her frown stayed fixed.

"So look, babe, I love you. And you know I would love to spend all night with you, but . . . well, I just want you to be safe, is all. And to do that, I had best keep you well clear of what all might be out here."

"What's out here?" she asked, looking out the window once more.

I wished I knew the answer to that, that was for sure. Could probably save me a lot of trouble one way or the other. "I don't know. Maybe nothing, maybe something."

"But something magic," she responded, still searching.

"Probably."

She turned back to me. "And you let me stay out here this long, why?" They were serious words, but said with a smirk.

I held up my beer can and grinned.

She slapped my arm then, pretty hard, laughing as she did so. Then she grabbed me by the front of my shirt and pulled me in for a deep, long kiss. Her hand began to roam up the inside of my thigh and soon enough found its way to the zipper of my pants. She tugged me free, taking me in her hand, and began to work it back and forth.

Then she pulled free of the kiss and gave "li'l me" a polite pat on the head. "Run along now," she purred in my ear.

I looked to my crotch, then back up at her. She made a little shooing motion with her hands, a wicked smile on her face. I laughed, trying to tuck myself away. "You dirty tease!" I hissed, snatching another kiss from her. I kissed her deep, our tongues meeting. With my free hand I grabbed the last beer.

"Bye, now," I said, escaping into the dark with my treasure. I heard her little bark of surprise as she saw the beer gone, but I knew she wasn't going to come into the rain to get it back. Sure enough, I heard her laughing, a faint sound mostly drowned out by the rain.

With a tiny rumble she cranked the car, and then she was gone.

And I was alone again, in the dark.

It Can't Rain All the Time

I finally saw that famous Norris temper in full effect when Earl showed up the next morning. It had rained for a good four hours, at least, once Anna had left, and the ground was basically a mudhole. It was bad enough that the man had left his truck on the dirt road, afraid that his truck might end up getting bogged down in the mud.

"I watched the weather last night!" he was shouting. "No rain forecast till late next fucking week! And it's dry as a fucking bone everywhere I drove this morning, except this one fucking patch!"

That . . . was not good. I'd just assumed that it had rained everywhere—you know, as rain does. If Earl wasn't being a hyperbolic twat and was correct that it had only rained here, then it was pretty clear to me that magic was at work. Magic that would need to be actively stopped, not just passively watched like the current plan.

Earl stomped over to where I was leaned against one of the log trailers. He was jabbing his finger around in about every direction, cussing up a storm. He rounded on me. "This is the exact shit I called you in to stop! The exact shit. So fucking do something about it!"

I think history has shown that I am usually not the most levelheaded of sorts, and I don't typically respond well to being cussed at. But my mind was too busy gnawing over the future to really focus too hard on old Earl. "Yeah, yeah," I said, looking out into the woods. "I'll handle it."

"You better! Thick as this mud is, gonna take at least two days to dry out enough that we can get to work. Add any more, and it'll be end of next fucking week before I can get started. Every day we sit idle, that just eats up my profit. Much longer and I'm gonna be losing, you hear me?!"

Still looking out at the woods, I extended an open palm to the man. I did it knowing it was probably going to piss him off, but I figured my almost-polite ignoring of his ranting was about all the nicety I could muster. But I wanted my money, so as to soothe the direction my mind was taking me.

'Cause all signs pointed to me needing to go into the woods, which I one hundred percent did *not* want to do. There was some powerful magic up in there, and I didn't want to have to face off with it. My mind kept going back to the last time I got caught up in some fucky weather, which had led to me having a knockdown, drag-out fight with a pooka that left my uncle's van wrecked.

My friendship with my uncle was still a little strained from it all. Not that I was afraid of further wrecking it—we had a bond that usually transcended my fuckery—but I really just didn't want to bring up those memories if I could help it. So that meant if I was going to call in reinforcements, it was gonna have to be Krista, not Hubert Dale.

Which sucked, seeing as HD was a hell of a lot easier to work with.

The longer I stared, the darker those woods got. They were a shadowed place, made doubly so by last night's rain. The bark was soaked and dark, and the limbs hung heavy and wet with lingering rain. I did not want to go in there.

Then I saw a little glimpse of orange, and a thought came to me. "Who put up those little orange flags?"

Earl, who had been angrily thumbing through his wallet, paused and looked at me. "I did. I do pretty much all my own flagging."

"So what's back there, then? Out in the woods, I mean?"

The glance he cut me told me that his anger had far from passed but that he was considering the fact that I was at least thinking on things. And that he thought I was crazy, which I realize is a lot to impart in a look, but I fancy I'm pretty good at reading folks. At least the negative aspects. "Trees. A bunch of old trees, mostly oak. And the one little road, though it's not much to speak of, really."

So why was there a road, then, I wondered? "Where does the road go, then?"

He frowned at that. "Nowhere, I guess. I didn't really follow it much. It sorta curves up a bit, so the line I was flagging didn't stick to it. Why? You think it goes somewhere important or something?"

I did indeed. No one, or no thing, would bother mag-icking that powerfully unless there was something worth spending that kind of energy. Either the MacGregors had something back there, or something magic had moved in and set up shop. Neither appealed to me, but it would explain why something didn't want this plot cut. Cutting it down would expose something that didn't want to be exposed.

He had fished out the money by now, and I took it from him. "Remains to be seen, I reckon. How about you pick me up a couple hours early so as I can go give a little looksee before I start my watch?"

Earl nodded, slowly. "Alright, then. But no more rain, you hear?"

I just rolled my eyes and started walking to the truck. "Why the fuck don't you bring me a biscuit each morning?" was my tactful response.

And Everything That's Golden and Green . . .

E arl did as he was asked. Things had certainly cooled off between us, though. Not to say that we'd ever been friendly, but at least initially there had been a sort of polite truce in our interactions. But my sparkling personality had won out, as it always does, and I could feel the man operating in a bit of constant seething when he saw me now. Which, you know, water off a duck's back and all that.

Maybe I would fix things and he'd return to neutrality. Or maybe not. Fuck 'em.

So it was that he dropped me off in the clearing well before it was set to get dark. And though he probably didn't realize it, I was HUMMING right along. I had forgone sleep in favor of a bewildering cocktail of goodies that I had used a fair portion of his money to buy.

Well, I mean, he probably had a little bit of an idea. The whole twitchy, not sitting still, drugged-up look was a bit of a clue, I would imagine. That's the thing about heavy drug use—you never have it as together as you think you do. So while I was feeling pretty jazzed up, shall we say, it wasn't without a cost, I reckoned.

I was tired, but not sleepy. Unless something dramatic happened, I probably wouldn't sleep for a couple more days, what with all I had taken. But all that just sort of masks the wear on your body, if that makes sense. I would eventually crash, and crash hard, but for now I was the goddamn Energizer bunny.

Watching Earl leave, I wished, and not for the first time, that I wasn't alone for this. I could maybe have browbeat Krista into coming, but I knew that if I played that card too early, I wouldn't have it up my sleeve later if I really ended up needing it. Besides, the goal here was simple reconnaissance, not a full-blown invasion. I just wanted to know what I was up against, was all. And besides, I had my cane pole if I needed it.

I paused at the edge of the wood. Even with the sun still up and out, it didn't look all that inviting. Earl wasn't lying—that was an old patch of woods. I had my doubts it had ever so much as seen an axe, other than for making the road through. The road was a narrow gash, like a wound that had never been allowed to fully heal.

Nature was trying, though, I found as I started to walk along its length. The grass was high, up over my knees, and sadly still a bit damp from last night's rain. Within a dozen yards I was pretty well wet, my cutoff jean shorts and wore-out Chucks soaked through. Every few feet there was some sort of shrub or bush trying to grow, most of which I could tell had been knocked over when Earl had come through on his truck at some point, but they had mostly righted themselves by now. Another five or six years and I reckoned you would never know this road was here at all, other than the fact that no fat oaks filled it.

It made me start to wonder . . . the MacGregors, far as I knew, hadn't really been back in years. *Years* and years. And while it was pretty clear this road hadn't seen recent use, it had at least seen some in the past few years. Otherwise, it would be even more overgrown.

The implication, my drug-addled mind said, was that the MacGregors had been slinking down here secret-like for some time, gotten what they needed, and then stopped coming.

Or, more troubling, maybe they had been run off. Given the two options, guess which my paranoid mind decided was more likely? I started running through a laundry list of the sort of bad things that could cause a bunch of folks with more power than me to decide to give an area a wide berth and, shockingly, nothing good came to mind.

It would have been best to not think like that, but when the drugs are flowing, let's just say you don't have the fullest control over the ways your brain turns and churns. So, of course, I honed in on every possible nasty I could think of and started eyeing which trees would be big enough that they could be hiding behind them.

And that was the thing about this patch of woods—those trees were BIG. I mean that. There were some oaks in there that could have easily hid that fat old satyr, the King, behind them with room to spare. I'd only ever seen trees like this once or twice in my life, and only in the deepest parts of the woods.

The deeper I got, the more I found that this little road didn't so much cut through the woods as it meandered its way along, threading around the biggest of the trees. That's the thing with trees that large—they have a way of choking out smaller life around them, soaking up all the resources. There were car-sized gaps in most of the areas, and it was through some of those gaps that the road went. What had initially been a cut road quickly became a thing much more a part of nature. Or a product of man's inherent laziness. Potato, potahto.

Overhead the limbs intertwined, and even though it was still bright out, it was mighty shady under there. It was like it was forever dusk beneath the boughs of that grove, and it might have been a touch peaceful if I hadn't known that big magic was lurking there.

I finally managed to shake myself loose a bit and carried on along the road. I knew that walking along there in the open such as it was probably wasn't the best move. But I was sure as shit not going to go off-trail, at least not yet. Not unless I had to. That was how you got lost, and getting lost in those woods probably wouldn't end real good for me.

There was the occasional bit of flagging tape on some of the trees, but I began to notice that they were increasingly more spread apart. And the farther I walked, the more oddly they began to be placed. I saw them hanging at every imaginable height, and in every imaginable fashion. Which, granted, wasn't a lot, since there are only so many ways you can flag like that, but it was clear that Earl was either a lot more creative than I would have ever given him credit for or that something had been affecting his mind in some way. I didn't know what he had been seeing, but I was pretty sure I was not seeing the same landscape he had been.

Was it the drugs? Had I drugged myself up to the point that the magic wasn't working on me as well? There was a chance of that, I thought. It actually had me feeling pretty good about it, like my drug use was working to my advantage in unintended ways. A little bit of my paranoia began to fade away. Like . . . I was *smarter* than whatever was out there. It needed to be watching out for me, and not vice versa.

And then I realized that somehow, following a more or less straight road that in no way looped, I had ended up right back where I started.

. . . Goes to Hell

I froze. I wasn't all the way back in the clearing, but I might as well have been. I was standing maybe forty feet from the exact spot where I had set out from, facing toward that small open expanse. Somehow I had gotten so thoroughly turned around that I hadn't even realized I was walking back down the road I thought I was walking up.

Fuck, I was high.

So, turning back around, I started walking up the road again, this time making damn sure to not get turned around. I made a point of keeping to the very right side of the path and reaching out to touch any trees that were close enough. You know, to keep me grounded. I couldn't really see the sun thanks to the thick limbs overhead, so as to make sure it was always in the same direction, but I could generally follow the light.

And then I was right back where I started again.

Now, yes, I was really, really high. There is no point in even trying to deny that. And sure, that didn't make me the picture of a proper woodland explorer. But fuck me, I tended to live in a perpetual state of being really high so long as the money lasted, and while no one really manages that state *too* well, I at least had years of experience.

Yes, it was possible I was too high to follow a road. It wouldn't be the first time. However, I was pretty sure that was not what was happening here. The paranoid part of my brain was back in charge now, telling me there was magic at work here. Something didn't want people reaching wherever that road went.

Which, let's be real, I didn't really want to reach the end of the road, either. But . . . I had to. That meant I was going to have to do a little extra, something I wasn't super excited to do. So, being me, I stood there smoking a cigarette while putting it off as long as I could. I don't know if there is a better taste on this planet than a nice, smooth menthol when you have other stuff you're putting off. At least not to me.

What finally got me moving was the fact that it would get dark, and as much as I didn't want to do a lot of things, walking around those woods at night was even lower down on that list. So after putting it off as long as I could justify, with one cig becoming two and then three,

I finally dug into my back pocket and pulled out a small ziplock bag.

I don't have a clue what you call these mushrooms, but they grow out in the grove behind Granny's. Most of the time, though, I got them from a guy my dealer Jimmy knows up in Montgomery. The first time I'd had one, it was one of my drunker nights I'd spent at HD's. I'd decided I was brave enough to sneak off back there and steal a few handfuls of these mushrooms. I'd known what they could do from when I was a little kid and had actually gotten a little magical schoolin', and I had, in fact, used them to, uh, decent(?) effect with that pooka mess, among other things. A few chomps, a few minutes, and then boom, you basically open your third eye.

It occurred to me this whole mess was becoming like some sort of reverse bizarro version of my run-in with the pooka. Instead of helping it rain, I was stopping it. Some weird magic was happening, and I was once again having to take these mushrooms to see it.

Ok, so maybe two minor parallels isn't a ton.

But still, it was enough to set me real on edge. That time had been rough, and I was loath to repeat it. My paranoia feelers were going nuts, to say the least.

There was no helping it, though. I popped a couple of the shrooms in my mouth, grit and all, and mashed them to paste between my teeth. They tasted like shit, and it was all I could do to not just spit them right on out. But I managed to swallow them, somehow choking them down without gagging too badly.

And then I started out into the woods once more, following along that little road. I knew that it wouldn't take long for the drugs to really kick in, and I had miles to go before I sleep, as they say. I wanted to get a jump on things and just banked on them kicking in before I got in too deep.

I knew things were beginning to happen when instead of getting darker as the sun started to set, it got brighter. It was subtle at first, but the farther I walked, the more it became clear that there was a glow about the place. Green. It was a green glow, the same color as those spreading root things I had seen that first night, and it was in everything, just slowly seeping out. I was in the middle of some magic grove, so full of magic that it had imbued the trees and plants with it. I saw a bird fly by and it was glowing, too. I just stared after it as it flew away, a thin misty green trail following in its wake.

About then is when I threw up.

I don't tend to focus much on it, but truth be told, drugs are kinda bad for you. Who knew? Ol' Nancy may have just been on to something. When you get bad on them like me, well, it's basically just a slow death. I liked to think I handled it better than most, and that I would be the one to beat the odds. Truth was . . . well, you lie to get yourself through the day. But who doesn't?

It took me a good long while to get it all out, and I would be lying if I said there wasn't a little bit of blood in the mix. But that's just the cost of doing business when you're a hero, I suppose. So there I was, on my knees, trying my best to keep it together with a magical wonderland exploding before my eyes. There was real beauty there, but I was too caught up being sick to give it the attention it deserved.

When I was done, I managed to fumble up some nearby plant to wipe my mouth with. It was like rubbing a glow stick across my face as, for a quick second, glowing leaves filled my vision. I was lucky, I decided. I could see little mashed-up chunks of mushroom on the ground before me, but seeing as I could still see the magic flowing around me, I wouldn't need to go "diving" for scraps, if you catch my drift.

Staggering to my feet, I tested the waters, as it were, to see if I was going to have another reaction. My throat wasn't closing up and my stomach had more or less settled, I decided. With a little shudder at the truly disturbing mound of refuse I was leaving behind, I set back off on my trek.

The spreading roots I had seen the other night had been thin; these were thick and broad. Clearly, the magic had been allowed to really dig in here and take root. Year upon year, something had been growing its magic until every tree, every animal was caught up in its net.

I turned to look back, and the sight sent a chill through me.

Clear as day, I could see each step I had taken going back about, oh, two dozen steps. The closer they got to me, the more withered and charred that magic aura looked. It was like every step I had taken was burning itself into the ground. Faint wisps of black floated up from the nearest imprints, as though the fresh char was dissipating on the wind.

But even as I watched, the green overpowered my steps, as if fresh grass was growing up in my wake. I looked down and took a step forward, then back. Sure enough, black holes in the aura appeared, but as I just stood and watched, if I waited long enough they "grew" closed once more.

I mean, I knew I was toxic, but this took that to a whole new level.

I shrugged it off. I didn't know what it meant, but I chose to not think about it. There were all sorts of implications there, but implications would be best handled over a few dozen beers with HD. For now, I had to focus on the problems in front of me, not behind, as it were.

Though I have many flaws and am lazier than most, walking does not bother me. Not having had a car in a long time, it didn't much faze me to walk most places. And I had to admit, walking through a wonderland of magic such as I was, well . . . there were a lot of worse things.

About a half mile up is where I hit the magic that had been fucking me up. With my magic eyes going, I could see it now for what it was, and I was fairly impressed. Stopping for what felt like the millionth time, I took a closer look. Essentially, it was a wall of illusion. I mean, it was nothing like what I could have made, but it also wasn't totally unlike the glyphs we'd put up the other day in a general sense.

Imagine a sea of glowing green shaped like trees and plants. Now start threading in some bits of glowing gold, like threads from a fraying carpet. The farther you walk into that weave of gold, the thicker it becomes. You look down and you see it starting to encase your legs, weaving itself around you.

Now imagine that all that gold created a sort of mirror image of the road stretching out before you, only with every step, it twists the golden road farther and farther. But since you have your magic eyes on, you can see the glowing green road, the actual road, beneath it. And because of that, you can keep walking along the path of green and stick to the actual path.

It was probably good that I had already thrown up, because that was one hell of a trippy view there for a bit. But as I kept to the verdant path, I could see those golden threads begin to rip and tear, and eventually it all just faded away. It was clever, mighty clever. But as I looked, I couldn't see any glyphs anywhere. Whatever I had just walked through, I guess it was some sort of, I don't know, natural defense? As natural as magic can get, I suppose.

Once I passed through that wall, the woods got a good bit thicker and, despite the glow, darker somehow. This was not a happy place, and as a guy who basically lives his life in a swamp of sadness, trust me when I say that.

In the Sun He Hides Away

I knew my time was shorter than I would have liked. Was I cursing my many starts and stops? Yes. Would it change my future behavior any? Unlikely. In fact, I didn't like the look of things ahead of me enough that I was already weighing another smoke break. But in a rare fit of "I'd rather not be yelled at because it started raining," I figured I could multitask. Shockingly, I am smart enough to smoke and walk at the same time.

I did have to stop to light it, though. Truth be told, it was all a little overwhelming. As I fished out my lighter and smokes, I eyed those woods warily. It wasn't like they felt evil or anything; they just felt . . . depressing. Like a lonely, forgotten place. Like they'd been so good at hiding themselves for so long that they had made themselves miserable.

When the cry came, I was so startled that I threw my lighter.

It was that same kinda loon cry I had heard the night of the coyotes, only now it was a whole lot closer, and with that proximity came clarity. It was a sad, lonely, pitiful sound. It ripped at me, and I'll be damned if I didn't start crying too. It crooned out, a wailing sound from an inhuman throat that quivered with abject bleakness and sorrow.

I wiped at my eyes, trying to clear them in case I needed to start running. Funny thing was, when that thing, whatever it was, made that sound, the whole forest seemed to get a little darker, and not just because we were starting to come up on dusk. No, it was like that cry sucked a bit of the energy from the place, and the glow faded just a little. Within a few seconds it had grown back, but it was a noticeable effect.

So whatever had made that sound, I gathered it was tied to the magic of this place. Not that I had suspected anything different, but it was nice to have confirmation, I guess—though I hate being right when it comes to magic, as it almost always comes back to bite me in the ass.

I figured whatever it was had to be pretty sizable. You didn't see squirrels out there making sounds that big, if you get my drift. No, that thing had some heft to it, and some damn big lungs. My hands tightened on my cane pole, then I laughed at myself. Was that laugh a bit manic? Maybe tinged with panic and hysteria, and fueled by paranoia? You bet your ass. What the hell would a stick, even if it was sorta magic, do against something like that?

Why the hell had I come into the woods with no gun? The fuck was wrong with me?

I didn't even try to find my lighter. Instead I just started slowly walking forward, trying to keep the terror at bay as I summoned up a bit of my power—you know, just to have it at the ready. And you know what? It did sorta settle me down a bit. Don't get me wrong, I was still a fucking mess, but calling on my power gave me something tangible to focus on, something I could do. And it helped.

Every step was leading me to something. I could see the glow grow stronger as I began to draw ever closer to whatever it was at the root of this whole thing. It didn't make things any brighter or any warmer, but it was like I could glimpse the building power. There was still that sad feeling in the air, and it, too, was getting stronger. All in all, not good.

I reached a little creek. It was only about ten feet across and not much more than calf deep, so no one had bothered to make any sort of bridge across it. The bottom was smooth with a few rocks, but none were high enough to keep me from getting my feet wet. Damn sure no way I was going to be able to jump it, not in my current state, so I just took the plunge.

The moment I was at the deepest part, I swear I felt the caress of some too-large catfish whiskers on my calf. I jumped, damn near killing myself as I scrambled out of the water. The touch had been electric, and not a little painful. Looking down, I could see several long thin lines of red that looked like I had been lashed hard with a switch.

Glancing back at the water for the briefest moment, I saw a giant dead-looking fishy eye staring back at me. It vanished as soon as I got a good look at it, but the point had been received. I had not been forgotten—I just wasn't needed yet. But soon.

It sent a chill through me, and I had to hold myself back from hurling some sort of magical blast in its wake. Not that I would have done any good, but I might have at least felt a little better about it all. There had been no humor in that eye, no mischief. Just a blank, cruel, uncaring gaze that cut right through me.

I made myself a promise I was not going to set foot in any more natural bodies of water, ever. How I planned to get back across the stream wasn't yet clear, but I would, well, cross that bridge when I came to it. Pun intended.

Leaning down, I took a gander at where my leg had been hit. None of the lashes broke the skin, thankfully, but they were starting to itch like the devil. It was like I had three big jellyfish stings, really, and seeing them through my mushroom eyes, I could make out the lingering touch of silvery black magic melting away from them.

They hurt like hell, but not enough to stop me from walking. I mean, not unless I wanted them to be enough. But I was starting to get angry—I had been at this for a couple of hours now and still hadn't gotten to the heart of the matter. I was hitting my limit for patience, that was for damn sure.

I really wanted a cigarette, but I had no way to light one now. I could have used magic, but I didn't want to be wasting my power on something petty when it could mean life or death any minute now. That just made me even more frustrated and angry.

The idea of just setting the whole woods on fire crossed my mind and, I will admit, lingered there a bit longer than it should have. If the whole point hadn't been to have some wood left to cut, I just might have done it. Instead, I just tried to soothe my rage by imagining the trees all aflame.

Then a branch poked me in the fucking eye.

I wasn't paying close enough attention and I'd walked too close to the edge of the road, which was getting steadily more narrow. Then boop—stick to the eye. It wasn't hard enough to do lasting damage, but damn, it hurt!

You know how you get mad and your clothes catch on something—in that way that *only* happens when you're fuming—and it just makes you irrationally angry even though it's just a real minor thing? That was me.

There was no thought behind it—it was all just an ingrained reaction, but I hit that sumbitchin' bush with a blast of magic, one hand cupping my eye, the other sending out raw energy. The green glow exploded from it as the bush was uprooted and hurled away from me. The bush turned black and took on a charred look, as if I had burned it up. I was pretty sure that was just magic visuals and that if I hadn't been tripping balls on shrooms, the shrub would've looked normal.

That visual didn't make me feel much better, but damned if blowing that bush away didn't make me feel like the king of petty mountain. My eye was watering up a storm, but at least that plant had gotten proper fucked. I almost didn't care about the magic I just wasted. I even did a real good job of convincing myself that the green glow surrounding me was getting darker because it had already been doing that, and not because I was burning through my shroom high first. I almost believed it.

Time was getting real short now. I wasn't sure if dusk would fall first or the shrooms would wear off, but I had to get a move on. I set off at a trot, deciding that there was going to be no more fucking around. In and out—quick, fast, and in a hurry. Running made me want to puke, of course, and my smoker's lungs were going to go into full revolt at any second, but I had made my bed through my usually fuckery, and I was gonna be forced to lie in it.

So, I ran.

How Have I Been Chased So Long

After a couple minutes of running, I came to a small clearing. It was big enough for a truck or two to park, or maybe just for one truck to turn around. As there was nothing there that I could see, I figured that this was the end of the road, at least when it came to vehicles. But you know, the thing about magic is that it rarely lives in super convenient public spaces, so I decided to pause and take a look around.

It took about half a minute for me to find what looked as though it might have once been a trail. That's actually what convinced me that it was what I was looking for—if it had the look of a place that got some use, then it was probably just a deer trail. So, I set off again.

It was more of a slow jog now. I was pressed for time, I knew it, but there simply was no running through this stretch. The trees were close and the brush was thick, and with it getting steadily darker, I knew that I risked getting lost if I wasn't careful. I was forced to sacrifice a little speed, though in truth my lungs thanked me, even if they still hated me.

I had only made it about a hundred feet or so when I figured out something was following me. Well, less following and more moving parallel to the path I was taking. It was a low shadow, and I knew better than to look at it dead-on. That would tip my hand, and I wanted to plot first. I called up my power, just a nudge, out of caution.

Discreetly, I tried to catch a slight glimpse without being too obvious about it. As it passed between two trees I saw a glimpse of gray-brown fur, just enough of a look to tell me what it was: a coyote. Which was not good. Any coyote I had ever seen should have been hightailing it away from me or, if it was rabid, maybe coming at me. But running alongside, all stalker-like? That meant hoodoo, even if I hadn't witnessed that scene the other night.

When I noticed another on my other side, I knew I was in big trouble. I couldn't help but think of that scene in *Jurassic Park* where the hunter guy, the one with the cool hat, got ambushed by a velociraptor. Clever girl, indeed.

If I lived, I promised myself I was gonna buy myself that hat. Even if it would cover some of my mullet, it was stylish enough to compensate, I reckoned. It would go damn well with my collection of Hawaiian shirts I had started to build.

I don't know how to describe it, but my magic eyes were fading yet the magic was getting brighter. Like, it was pretty clear I was getting close to the heart of things, but only as my magic was fading. Only it was fading at a slow enough rate that the strength of the glow kinda more than offset it. That was a good thing, I reckoned, because if I had hit it with my eyes at full zoom, then I might have been blinded, like looking at the sun too long. This place fucking oozed with old magic, built up over years upon years.

On an impulse I stopped, turning to start running back down the way I came. Not because I wanted to run away, even though I kinda did, but because I wanted to see what these coyotes would do. I could see those strange, weird charred footprints in my wake, though the farthest back were already fading away. Before I could start, though, a third coyote stepped into view.

It moved to block me, perhaps only thirty feet back. Its long tongue was lolling out, and I could see its toothy grin as it stared at me. It didn't move, it didn't make any threatening motions—it just stood there like it was going to stare me down. Looking left and right showed me that the others had paused, too, and were likewise looking at me, only now there looked to be shadows that might have meant more beasts.

I took a step forward and the coyote in front of me bristled, then loosed a low growl. That was all I needed. I could have blasted it with power, sure, enough to kill it easily. But could I get them all before one of them latched on to me? Iffy. I had no idea just how many there were, and not knowing made me real skittish.

So, I turned back around and set off one last time. At least that was the plan, but fuck me if I hadn't hit my limit for bullshit, even if it was mostly self-inflicted. I didn't bother jogging, though, not anymore. I knew I had to be getting close, and I didn't want to be winded when I got to . . . well, whatever was ahead.

The trees were growing ever more thick, both in their individual size and in number. Earl was going to make a fortune if he ever got a chance to get back here, but all that growth made for a lot of shadow and darkness. I lost sight of the coyotes for the most part, though I had little doubt they were still there. Not seeing them but knowing they were there really didn't help my paranoia any, and I kept looking back over my shoulder. I was convinced that at any second I was going to get pounced on, so I kept my power up and ready.

The glow was pretty much all gone now. I don't know if fear hurts my abilities, but I'm pretty sure it doesn't help. I was going to be going into things "blind," but honestly that didn't faze me too much. I had my doubts that there were multiple layers of confusion like what I had been caught up in earlier. What would be the point? Either someone could get past it, or they couldn't. If they could make it past the first time, then they were sure to be able to do the same a second time.

No, any other defenses were probably more . . . physical.

My eyes kept roaming left and right, trying to keep an eye on my coyote herders, so it took a second for me to realize that up ahead I could see a break in the trees. I instantly knew that whatever was there, that was what I had been questing for this whole time. My heart was pounding, and I think I was really on the verge of coming all apart emotionally. I had really done a number on myself with these drugs.

As I stepped into the clearing, my breath caught. It was—it was so beautiful.

The clearing wasn't too large, maybe a sixty-foot circle, thereabouts. The grass was so short cropped that it looked almost like someone had come along and cut it recently, only there were a number of mushrooms sprouting up in fairy rings that proved that to be impossible. Each of the mushrooms was a different color just about, all shades of browns and greens, a few with white or blue streaks in them. There were even a couple of orangey-gold ones in the mix, splashes of color that drew the eye.

But that was just the spice. The meat of things was the giant menhir smack-dab in the middle of things. It had to be at least ten feet tall, maybe eleven, and a good four feet across at the base. It was a slab of gray stone that was about a third covered with a patina of green lichen. I could see that there were a few glyphs and symbols carved into it, but I couldn't make out just what they were. Spirals seemed to be a theme, though, that much was clear.

There was a cleft at the top, and from it grew a small tree. Honestly, it made me think of a bonsai; it was only about three feet tall, but it looked fully formed and gnarled with age. Its leaves were such a dark green that they almost looked black, and I thought I could see some small green-gold berries growing on some of the branches. The roots of the thing were spreading out from the cleft, flowing down from the top of the stone like a spiderweb.

The sun was now setting behind the trees, but there was a moment, one absolutely perfect moment, where the setting sun was sinking behind that dwarf tree. The beams of light diffused through the glen, and everything was bathed in golden rays. I swore I smelled honeysuckle thick in the air and even had the taste of it rich on my tongue.

For a brief moment I got the impression that all of it—the stone, the tree, the glen—was more than what I was actually seeing. There was an echo in my eyes that made me think the tree actually towered far above me, and that the stone was more door than monolith. That behind it all there was something else, a second world, but I didn't have the key to open it. Instead, I could just sense its expanse, shut away from a pitiful little creature such as myself.

I felt small. Unworthy. This was a place of true power, likely once the heart of all the McGregor strength and a lodestone of the County. It was the kind of place for a true user of magic, not untrained would-be wizards hopped up on drugs.

A shadow appeared to the side of the monument, and in its wake came a massive shaggy head.

THE DEATH OF COYOTE WOMAN

Yellow-black eyes peered out at me as a horse-sized coyote came out from behind the menhir. It was so large that it would have been impossible for it to have hidden behind the monolith without me knowing it was there. It had clearly come from . . . that other place, wherever the menhir had locked away inside it.

Even with its large size, it still had that ranginess to it. Its legs were long, thinner than you would think, and its shaggy black-tipped tail swayed back and forth with each step. Its head was hunched low, its large mouth closed and ears forward. It was eyeing me up, and clearly wasn't afraid. Not that it had any reason to be. My head would easily fit inside its mouth, I reckoned.

But beyond its size, there was something off about this beast. It looked sick, somehow. Its eyes were more jaundiced than golden, and there were patches of fur that looked so thin as to be almost mangy. Coyotes are a thinner sort of creature than, say, wolves, but this one looked downright gaunt. I thought I could see some bones jutting out, pressing against its skin.

As we faced off I could see the rest of the coyotes, all normal sized, come out of the woods in their ones and twos until there was a pack of at least a dozen lining the edge of the glen. They sat on their haunches, none of them bothering to look at me. All eyes were on the massive beast before me.

I could see that it was a she, as it looked as though it had been nursing at some point in the recent past. The thought of there being more critters this size was equally nightmarish, but that was a problem for tomorrow Marsh, if he was blessed enough to exist in a couple of minutes. Maybe that explained why it looked so sickly, but something told me that wasn't the case.

Terrified, I managed to hold it together. I had no doubt that a thing like that could probably smell the fear on me, but I hoped the fact that I didn't just bolt and run might do me some small favor. I called up my magic for real now, holding it ready to blast out at this monster the moment she stepped wrong. I had no idea if it would work, but I knew damn well I would go down fighting and cursing. Daddy didn't raise me to be afraid of a scrap, the bastard.

The coyote sniffed deeply, a move that felt more human than beast. Her head cocked to one side, and in my head I could hear her words. *You are no McGregor.*

That put a right fear into me, no lie. Animals that could talk, like freaky-giant catfish, for example, rarely did me any good. They almost always were trouble of a magnitude larger than I would ever want to deal with. The fact that you could reason with a critter like that very rarely meant you actually would succeed.

Still, I had been pretty sure that this was McGregor turf, even if they had abandoned it. It was nice to know I'd been right. What really hit me, though, was the haunted tone of those words. They were filled with a loneliness, a sorrow that cut me deep. I didn't cry, but I sure wanted to. My throat grew a little tight, and not just from being scared.

It was a sadness that I felt echoing deep in me. I knew that kind of sorrow, even if I didn't want to admit it. "I'm not." I said it out loud, not having any clue how to speak with my mind like this creature. I don't think the sadness came through in my voice, or at least I tried not to let it.

You stink like a Marsh. But I have not smelled you before.

There was definitely some animosity in the way she said my last name, the only brief respite from the sorrow. But luckily, a lifetime of experience had caused me to pretty much always expect that tone when people said my name. "Well, I reckon that's because I am one, and we haven't had the pleasure, I don't believe. So who the fuck are you?"

For a second the fur around her neck bristled, and she took a short step toward me. She was touchy, that was clear. Which was probably a bad thing, but maybe I could work it to my advantage. An angry mind wasn't the clearest thinking, I knew well.

A scared one wasn't, either, but there was nothing I could do about that.

Where are the McGregors? Where is the Old Marsh?

The Old Marsh was what folks had called my grandpa. And he certainly wasn't coming around anytime soon, seeing as he was kinda dead. Mostly. "The McGregors aren't coming. They've moved to the big cities, and they ain't looking to come back. Hell, they sold this place to get the timber cut, make a few bucks to pay for some big party, no doubt."

Lies. They would never hurt their Grove. The scruff rose once more, and I could see some bared fangs, hints of yellowed white that looked about the size of my fingers. It took all I could muster to not flinch back.

I mean, what do you say to a giant fucking coyote that's calling you a liar? I wasn't lying, but I didn't think that really mattered. So I decided to stick to the truth, which was sorta a new approach for me. "I think you know I'm not lying. And I think you're the one who's been fucking up my boss's plans to cut this timber. Keeping it raining and such. The one who sent all those critters after me the other night. That about the size of it?"

She just kept snarling at me, which I took as a yes. "When was the last time you even saw a McGregor coming up here? Been years, ain't it? They've moved on, and I reckon they're trying to destroy anything they left behind that could be used to hurt 'em. Or maybe they're just trying to get rid of the evidence that maybe their rise to power wasn't on the level. Either way, they want this place mowed down. So, you're fucked."

The magic is strong. It will protect this place as it has for generations.

I laughed at that. "I think you're thinking of some other place. This is Jubal County, not the fucking old country. Everything turns to shit here. We're the shittiest county in a shitty state. The only thing that's grown here is poverty, but damn if we don't have a bumper crop of that."

The agitation coming off the big coyote was infecting the little ones. A couple had stood up, and several more I could see were squirming a bit. One even wined for a second, before the she-coyote looked its way. That shut it up quick. *Why are you here?* she hissed at me. At least I think that was the tone she was going for. This mental talking stuff was kinda weird.

I gave a little shrug, all noncommittal-like. Like this was no big thing, just another Saturday in the County. Fake it till you make it, I always say. "For right now, I need to stop it from raining. Longer term, I guess I need to evict all y'all to someplace else so my boss can cut this timber."

No. All the coyotes were on their feet now, and Big Momma had every one of her fangs bared.

"Hey, now!" I shouted. "Everyone be easy!" My hands erupted into light as I called up some power to hurl at whoever moved first. My blood felt electric. We were dancing on a knife edge, and at any moment everything was about to go sideways. The sort of sideways that ends with me six feet under, or in a pile of coyote crap.

Two things happened almost at once. To my left, one of the normal coyotes started to dart forward, its mouth open in a snarl. It was like time slowed there for a split second, allowing me to see that beast in way too much detail, an arrow of fur and fangs bearing down on me.

And I messed up.

But you can't really blame me; reflex is a bitch. I started to turn to blast the critter away before it could attack me.

And when I did that, I didn't really stop to think just what sort of reach a monster the size of the she-coyote could have, how it would really only take one good step for her to be on me.

So that little coyote drew my eye, and in that split second Big Momma jumped forward and, with a mouth full of far too many teeth, snatched me up by my arm.

Her teeth buried themselves in my arm, so quick it was like a snake strike. I could feel her fangs parting skin and felt that sickening *click* as they snapped closed around the bone. With a flick of her head, I was sent ragdolling into the air as if I weighed less than nothing. I was screaming, I knew that, and even though she let go, I knew my arm was broken. I heard it snap like a twig, broken in two places, the sound somehow breaking through the shrieks pouring out of me. The damn thing flopped like a broken wing, and as I went flying I felt a splatter of my own blood land hot and sticky across my face.

I was hurled skyward, an impossible motion, easily ten, fifteen feet in the air. I was higher than the menhir, and for a split second the sun came back into view as I rose. My body spun as I twisted in a vain attempt to make it so I could land on my hands—rather, hand and feet. But as I turned, it was not the ground I saw below me.

That coyote queen had opened her mouth, and to match my impossible height she had stretched it to an impossible width. There was no tongue, no fangs—not anymore. There was nothing between the thin pink-black gums, a bottomless emptiness. It was a void, and it was stretching wide to swallow me up. She was a big critter, but a moment ago she hadn't been close to being able to swallow me whole . . . and now there was room to spare.

I thought about trying to blast my power at her, but I was in far too much pain. I couldn't manage even to stop screaming, much less harness the powers of eldritch might. Instead, I did the only thing I could manage to do.

I fell.

And the void enveloped me like a lover's embrace.

Oh, They're Reckless, and Baby, So Weary

I heard her jaw snap closed. I would say I heard it behind me, but it sounded more like it was all around. A moot point either way, as I was hurtling through an inky black void. I very much had a sense of falling, though with utter blackness on all sides it felt totally surreal. I had no concept of up or down, just that I was falling in a direction, so that had to be down.

I didn't really have an arm anymore. I just had a pain appendage, something that flopped limply and made me scream whenever it bumped into anything. It was bleeding badly, but I didn't think I could muster up the wherewithal to try and stop the bleeding just then. That would mean putting pressure on the broken bone, and I thought I would probably pass out if I tried.

With a breath-stealing thud, I landed. I would have screamed as I landed on my arm, but again, no breath. I think I blacked out for a second as the pain overwhelmed me, and it was only gasping for air and sobbing that brought me back.

I fought to sit up, and as I did my surroundings hovered into view. I was in a twisted reflection of where I had just been, I thought, though there was more here than where I was before. It was clear I wasn't in Kansas anymore, thought Toto.

The sky was stormy, heavy with thick purple-black clouds. There was an almost constant rumble of distant thunder, and flashes of light cut the sky every few seconds. There was no rain, not yet, but you could feel it coming. The air seemed pregnant with it, but instead of being that cool, refreshing feeling before a summer storm, this felt dank.

I was in a grove, though this one was bigger, maybe four, five times the size, and instead of one stone pillar there were several. One was the exact twin of what I had seen in the real world, and it was just off to my left—small tree, spirals, the works. Identical.

There was another menhir I recognized. It was not as tall as the one beside me, but it was a bit more broad. It had glyphs carved on to it, too, glyphs I knew all too well, seeing as they were scarred onto my chest. That would be the stone that sat at the center of Granny's grove, I thought, though I hadn't been there in daylight in many a year. And the few times I'd been there at night, I'd been more focused on stealing shrooms than actually taking a look around. At the very least, it matched what I could remember.

There were others, however. One, the smallest, was covered with sigils that looked like a bird, I thought. A second looked like it had been struck by lightning and was more a pile of rubble than an actual standing stone. A third wasn't stone at all; it was a wooden cross that had been charred and burned but was still intact somehow. And there were a host of other ruins that I thought maybe looked like they could've been Native American. They had clearly seen better days.

Granny's stone, and that squat birdy one, they sorta glowed a little. Just real faint-like, though Granny's was the brightest. I would describe the light coming from my family's stone as, well, baleful. It wasn't a heartwarming glow at all, sorta a purple-and-red swirl flecked with a rotten-looking black. The other one was more orangey-yellow, but it also had bits of black in it besides, being so faint that it was hard to see. If it had been full day in wherever this was, I don't think I could have; the gloaming did it a favor in that regard.

But you know what? Fuck all that. I didn't care that I was in a magical wonderland of fairy fucking delight. My. Arm. HURT.

For the first time I was able to look at it, and what I saw made me want to vomit. I could see bone, and broken bone, at that. Red, though, was the primary color as blood poured from the wounds the fangs had inflicted. I needed to get it wrapped, and the only thing I had was my shirt. I knew getting it off was going to be a bitch, though.

I cried a bit as I got my shirt off, and I was thankful that except for the blood, this was a pretty clean shirt—for me, that is. But easing it down and off my shattered arm was one thing. Wrapping said arm was another.

I did it, though, somehow. I flirted with fainting again, and there was much ado, much wailing and gnashing of teeth, as the preachers would have said. The shirt was quickly soaked with blood, and it did basically nothing for the broken nature of it, but it was the best I could do.

Arm wrapped, I looked up for the first time in several minutes, surprised to find I wasn't alone anymore.

You're Dead and Out of This World

In the midst of all the stones there was a spectral figure, ghostlike and pale. Its body was human enough, but its head was a shifting swirl. One minute it looked like a coyote or wolf, then the next second it looked more like some sort of bird, then it would shift into a broad-antlered deer. But in whatever form it held, the eyes stayed the same. They were dark, impossible swirls, like a pair of black holes coming to life. They were the opposite of light, and it seemed as though they sucked in the gloaming around it, giving the already spectral form an even more shadowy blur to its edges.

Paying it attention was clearly where I fucked up. Our eyes met, such as they were, and after a few seconds of met gazes, it started to stalk angrily toward me, its hands forming the sort of complex motions that magic called for. It was summoning up big magic, and it sure wasn't trying to hide that fact.

In all my screaming and almost dying, I hadn't had a chance to shoot my wad with all this power I had summoned up. And yeah, I had a broken flipper, but hell, I hadn't ever learned magic right in the first place. I couldn't do what this thing could, but I bet it hadn't ever lived anything like the fucked-up life I had.

With my good arm, I hurled out the power I had called up. My arm erupted in a gout of light as a burst of fire came roaring out. Without using both my arms like I should have, it hurt—it hurt a fucking lot, in fact. All the hair on my arm burnt off in an instant, and I could feel the heat strong on my arm, to the point I knew I was gonna have some damn pink skin in a second.

It hit that creature and rocked the thing back. It had to stop its casting to cross its arms and throw up a quick ward, faster than I could have, I noticed with a fair bit of dismay. I could see that it had caught fire in some places, which was the real takeaway here. Ghosts don't catch fire, in my experience, so if it could burn, I could kill it.

I was already moving, though. I needed to get some into some cover, fast, and start calling up more power. I had a fair bit in the tank—I had taken a whole lot of drugs for just this event—but I was sure that it would have more. *Everyone* had more. I needed to put it down fast.

The nearest cover was the spiral-covered menhir, so I made a dash to get behind it. Being a squirrely little shit, I fit behind it easily, and with one eye peeking out, I started getting that electric tingle brewing as I brought up more of my power. I wanted to blast the void eyes right off that thing, and I knew I was gonna have to use up a huge chunk of what I had left to do it.

The thing hadn't bothered trying to put out the flames. The great thing about magic fire is that if you don't do something about it, it's gonna keep burnin', and burnin' hot. So it was fucking up, I thought, because the alternative would be that burning up wouldn't actually stop it, and that didn't bear thinking about.

It was coming toward me once more, only now its eyes, which had been two black pools, now were tinged with red. I guessed that meant I had pissed it right off. But I had called up about all the power I could handle at once, and with a cry I stepped out from behind the stone and sent a blast of raw energy toward the thing, enough to drop a herd of bulls, I reckoned. But I'm not left-handed . . .

The blast, instead of rocking its head clean off, struck the monster's right leg. It hit at the knee, blowing away a huge chunk of spectral flesh. The thing spun half around and fell to the ground, but fuck me if, in spite of all, it never took its eyes off me. And the way it fell, it actually fell closer to me. Before I could duck back behind the rock, it lashed out with one arm.

The arm reached out, and as it did, it stretched its length till it was long enough to reach me. It was like grasping vines, and it snarled itself around my ankle. It was hot, almost to the point of burning, and as it drew tight on my flesh I could feel it tearing a bit with one hell of a friction burn. I tried to hop away, snatching at my leg to try and free it so I could get behind cover, but it was way too strong. I started to call up some more power with an intent to blast the damn arm away, but then it tugged.

I fell hard, and even though I didn't land on my broken arm, it did flop into the ground. I felt bone grind against bone, and I screamed. Somehow I didn't pass out, even though I wanted to. Really, I just wanted it all to be over. If I wasn't so fucking contrary, I might have just let the thing finish me then, without so much as a fight. God, I was so tired. Life was just so fucking heavy.

But I thought of Anna. And I fought.

The thing hadn't tried to stand. Instead, it was crawling toward me in a strange hopping lope, like a three-legged dog. Those eyes never stopped boring into me, and as it came forward it also tried to pull me toward it. I saw a mouth form below that swirling nothingness, and it was full of needle-thin teeth through which flowed an acrid, foul-smelling breath. It was the scent of decay and rot, of soured flesh left too long on the roadside.

With the power I had summoned, I managed a working somehow. Sitting on my ass, one-armed, and being pulled toward my death, I was able to piece together the motions, and with a shout I managed to blast that grasping arm. Months of actually trying to get better at what I do was coming in clutch. It wasn't as direct a hit as I would have liked on the arm, but the rest of the force of that blow lashed back and smacked the thing right in its mouth, and I saw a dozen teeth explode.

The hand around my ankle turned loose, just enough that I could pull myself free. I hastily stumbled to my feet as I tried to get behind the menhir and out of sight. I just needed a second, and if you thought I was above the whole "racing around the dinner table" strategy of keeping that big rock between me and it, well, you would be dead wrong.

I made it, though I felt that thing's hand go whooshing just behind me as it tried to snatch me up once more. But a heartbeat later I was behind the stone and, for a split second, free to try and regain some balance. Turning, I could see that the arm was still stretching out, but it was starting to recoil. I could hear the creature scrabbling across the ground, heading my way, but it wasn't in sight yet.

Bringing up my power, I knew I had enough for one more real big blast. Beyond that . . . it was iffy. And it's not like I had time just that second to try and do a quick rail off the back of my hand, even if I could fish the needed drugs out my back pocket.

I was crying, both in pain and fear. I knew this was probably going to be bad, but I didn't really think death was the sort of magnitude of repercussions I might deal with. I mean, sure, there was always a chance, but fuck me, there's that chance every time I do drugs and it doesn't stop me. But this whole cursed thing, it was just about cutting some fucking trees! All I wanted was to escape, and get back to Anna.

Anna.

Nothing like death to show you what really matters. If I lived, I vowed to be better. To deserve her. To not be an absolute piece of shit.

I had to live first, though.

I took a second and tried to center myself. I took my good hand and frantically pawed at my eyes, clearing them so I could make the most of this shot. There was no controlling my breathing; I was having a full-blown freak out, but I did the best I could. My heart was pounding so loud, it drowned out the near-constant thunder, almost covering the sound of that thing coming for me.

Arm raised, I stepped out from behind the stone, only a little, just enough that I could take a shot. But I fucked up. I had taken too long, I found, as the thing was close, far too close. Its hand was already raised and it clamped its rough hand around my throat, slamming me into the stone.

It had gotten to its feet, using one too-long arm as a crutch for its shattered leg. But that left one hand free to strangle me as it drew closer with its rows of too many teeth. All of which was really pressing, but fuck if I wasn't on the verge of going under as my broken arm struck the stone. I saw a splatter of blood rain over the stone as my arm hit it, my shirt having soaked all the way through by now.

The hand around my throat was so large, its vine-like fingers so lengthy, that only part of it was actually wrapped tightly around my windpipe. The rest of the hand pinned my shoulder and upper arm to the stone, preventing me from making the motions I needed, not that I could even begin to focus well enough to try. Blackness was coming, dragging me down into the abyss of death.

I had no air, but it was all too much. It was impossible to scream, to work my magic, to do anything. So I didn't scream . . . but I did? Does that make sense? Everything in me, all the anger, the sadness, the power, it all came racing up in a torrent, and somehow I screamed it out, even though I had no air.

It was a song of pure anguish, as terrible as it was mournful and twice as angry. And with it came up every last bit of power I had hoarded up. It poured out of me in a wave, crashing into anything around me, which was mostly stone and monster. The stone didn't give . . . but the creature did.

With a roar of its own I saw it stagger back, turning me loose. I slid down the stone, my arm flopping against the structure and smearing a bloody streak down its length as I collapsed into a gasping puddle at the base. That thing, though, had it worse.

The power slammed into it, knocking it back a good half dozen steps. It wobbled on its "crutch," but it couldn't hold itself up and went crashing down. Its spectral flesh was flayed, peeling back the flesh to the bone in places and dimming those baleful eyes. Its already blasted leg broke completely in twain, severing itself just below the knee.

If I could have breathed normally, I might have breathed a sigh of relief at having taken the thing out of the game. But I was still trying to catch my breath at all, and my hitching lungs wouldn't let me do anything but gasp as they tried to fill themselves back up. I couldn't even stand to try and make sure the thing was dead, and even if I could have . . . I was totally spent. There was not a whiff of power still lingering in my veins.

And then the thing sat up.

I'm not gonna lie—I gave up just then. It wasn't like I could do anything against it; I could barely breathe, and I damn sure didn't have the magic for a working. As the thing got slowly to its foot and hands, I just sat there uselessly. I thought about trying to crawl away, but then I remembered my broken arm. I didn't even try. I looked up, into the stormy heavens above me, and wished a lightning bolt would just come finish the job.

I could see the blood that I had shed on the stone was filling up the spirals that had been carved into it. The blood was steadily being sucked into the center of those spirals, like some sort of bizarre stone straw. "Fuck me .. . even the rocks . . . are bloodthirsty . . . here," I whispered between gasps.

A second later, there was a dull whomp. Roiling out from the stone behind me came a wall of power that struck the creature head-on. It was blasted apart, disintegrating into a pile of dust that was just as quickly blown away. It didn't have time to whimper, much less loose a death rattle. One second it was there; the next it was gone.

At the same time, I was doubled over in a staggering amount of pain as my chest erupted in agony. I had felt this pain before, twice, and I knew it well. But this pain shouldn't have been possible, as there was no hot iron brand being pressed against the flesh of my chest, as my grandparents had done when I was a child.

Hunched over as I was, though, I could see that there was a bubbling and charring on my chest as some invisible force branded a spiral sigil in the center of my chest. I watched in screaming agony as the brand gouged my skin deep, then began to instantly scar over. It was the entire branding and healing process combined into an eternity about ten seconds long.

Coupled with that torment was the fact that I could see the scars of my older brands fading at the same rate. I was far beyond thought as this was happening, of course—I was just trying to not totally destroy my vocal cords with screaming, and fighting to keep from fainting. I was mostly successful on the first, but as soon as the worst of the pain stopped and the new glyph healed itself, the sweet release of unconsciousness consumed me.

Fruitful Harvest in a Wicked Garden off a Forbidden Tree

It didn't rain that night. Or the next.

In fact, it didn't rain once ever again as Earl Norris cut the ever-lovin' hell out of that stretch of timber. And really, it was all thanks to me, and I made sure Earl knew it. And you know what, I think he was actually thankful. Like, genuinely so.

I say that because he did what I asked him to do, which was take that big machinery of his, load that menhir up, and tuck it away safe in some barn he owned. Because one day, I was gonna come calling for it.

He balked a bit at first, seeing as he was already covering my doctor's visit to get my arm fixed. But then I told him that what he wanted, his dream—it was gonna take that stone. I just was gonna need a place to put it, and then . . .

Fuck, I don't know. I woke up and all the magic that had been oozing out of the menhir into the surrounding area had vanished, sucked up back inside it, I reckoned. I was its servant now, I gathered . . . but I hadn't the first fucking clue what that meant.

I did know three things, though.

First, and most important, was that I wasn't tied to Granny anymore like I had once been—and I knew she wasn't going to like that. Not at all. Granny was greedy, and I knew there would be hell to pay sooner rather than later.

Second, that I loved Anna like I hadn't loved anyone in a long, long time. And seeing her face as she came to pick me up from the urgent care clinic was the happiest I had been in a long time. Happy enough to maybe make me try to be a little better, at least for a week or two.

And last, I knew that wiping my face with poison ivy after puking had been a bad, bad call, even if I hadn't realized it at the time. But don't worry—I became aware all too soon.

Fuck my life.

Epilogue

Blood splattered against the wall, a crimson rain doing its best to impersonate a Jackson Pollock painting. The ancient cellar walls seemed to soak it up hungrily, and a few moments later it had disappeared. Granny didn't notice; her focus was on the carcass before her.

The sound of heavy work boots on old wooden stairs caused her to glance up briefly, even though she knew by the sound of the tread who it was. Sure enough, her oldest son, who most everyone called Black Tom, was coming into view. If he was disturbed in the least at the sight of his mother up to her elbows in the gaping guts of a deer, he didn't show it.

Granny went back to rummaging around within the carcass. Tom knew better than to bother her while she was like this, so he maintained his distance, leaning easily against the wall where, moments before, the blood had landed. He stood with a preternatural stillness, a trait that never failed to unsettle most anyone around him.

Granny, however, was not most people. She was likely the only person more intimidating in Jubal County, despite her age and relative frailty.

With a triumphant shout, she pulled out some part of the deer's viscera. She sat it to the side for later inspection—the augury could wait until she had Tom squared away, she decided. Besides, like all her family, she wanted to keep him in the dark as much as possible. Tom might be the one most like her, if not for his total lack of any sort of magical ability, but that didn't mean he needed to know all her machinations.

Grabbing up a much-stained rag, she started to wipe as much of the blood from her arms as she could, stepping around the table as she did. "You took your sweet time getting here. I called for you three weeks ago."

Tom just stared back at her, unmoving. She knew him well enough to know that he'd have a good reason for not coming running the moment she called. Still, the thought of it grated on her nerves. "It's about your boy."

Tom's face turned into a hate-filled grimace. "What's the little shit done now?" he spat.

"He tried claiming the McGregor's stone. And for some reason, it let him." She paused to let that sink in. Tom's eyes arched, making it clear he understood the import. "He's gone too far this time. I don't know if it was by mistake, or planned—you never can tell with Howard. But we can't risk it. I need him gone, and soon."

"Gone and buried?" Tom asked, his tone making it clear that was what he wanted. There was no love lost between father and son, and it would be far from the first time he'd had to hide a body.

Shaking her head, Granny tossed the bloody rag onto a pile of similarly soiled cloth. "No, not yet. He still has his uses. I just want him gone for a bit. Pile on some stress on him so he'll crumple under it, like always, and wind up back in a bad enough way that any thought of learning and growing his craft will become a distant memory. You'll think of something."

"Aight, then. I'll make it happen. I got a run west coming up pretty soon—I'll do it then. I'll need to keep low till then, though. I got a little more heat on me than normal."

Granny just turned and walked over to where the bloody organ of the deer lay. His dismissal clear, Tom stalked out of the cellar, leaving his mother to her witchcraft. On the table the deer shuddered once, bleating weakly, before finally dying.

THE BACK MATTER!

About the Author

Born and raised in South Alabama, Bob is an author, podcaster, tabletop game designer, and all around hot mess. His cause of death will most likely result from one of the hitchhikers with he picks up reckless abandon. A study in contrasts, he once skinny-dipped at a wedding and is also an Eagle Scout. He has two useless college degrees, has roadied for bands, and broke his wrist in a wall of death at a Divine Heresy show. He's written for video games, designed board games, and owns a disturbing number of roleplaying games. When he was eight he give a camel a coke in Israel and got flashed in Paris. When he grew up he watched a monkey steal a man's wallet in Costa Rica. He's made passible podcasts, filmed terrible short horror movies, and been the producer on a trio of albums you've never heard of. Thriving on the groans of those he has punned around he spends far too much time nervously laughing. He once dug up a dead cow in a creek thinking it was a human cadaver and has a cousin that's a water witch. In college he gave haunted ghost tours (even though he's pretty sure ghosts aren't real). He's been stalked, gave a Prophet a lift, and been stagger drunk in more states than he would care to admit.

Growing up, he was always jealous of the wide variety of jobs his favorite authors listed in their 'about the author' sections, not fully realizing what a hellscape he was lusting after. So to that end Bob has been in no particular order: a warehouse clerk, a roadie for a band, pizza delivery guy, grocery store bag boy, telephone survey giver, inventory manager, quit Walmart after only three days, and currently works in IT. Learn from him sweet children, and flee now to the woods and leave behind the world of men.

More relevant he wrote this book, some other books, and has been published by a number of other folks with questionable judgement. The fictional things he writes sometimes come weirdly true. He lives in the middle of Alabama with his amazing LadyWife, the Kiddo, and a number of increasingly portly cats.

You can learn more at **www.talesbybob.com**

Reviews!

Did you leave a review? In the immortal words of Mathew McConaughey: "It'd be a lot cooler if you did."

Email List!

If you want to keep up with news about my books, this is the best way! I'll never sell or share my email list, and I promise to never bother you more than once a month (unless, like, its super-mega-secret important). To sign up go to my website: **www.talesbybob.com**

Patreon!

If you want even more Bob content, then go check out his Patreon. It's full of short stories, flash fictions, even draft copies of books. Big news also gets announced there before anywhere else, along with sneak peaks of book covers and other behind the scenes content. A popular series on there are 'The Marsh Dispatches' which is an ongoing series of essays written from the perspective of Howard Marsh the Methgician. Check out **www.patreo n.com/talesbybob**

Transparency!

When I started out, I had no other authors that I knew well enough to ask questions about sales numbers, social media growth, etc. I had no idea if my sales numbers were good, bad, or somewhere in-between. But seeing as I'm a big believer in the concept of '*be the change you want to see*' I started sharing all that information in hopes that it would motivate other authors to do the same. And even if they don't, at least this information is available to anyone who wants to know what those types of stats look like for a small time author like myself. So if you visit my website you can see all sorts of behind the scenes information each month, like how my social media grew (or shrank), how sales were, what I tried differently that month, etc. I also break down my stats around my book launches and get into the nitty gritty of each major in person event I do. Check out **www.talesbybob.com/transparency-project**

Education!

I have been helped by countless other creatives and authors along my journey. So anything I can do to pay that help forward, I do. That's why as much as possible I try to keep a host of free resources on my website folks to learn from. If I get paid to teach a workshop, I usually turn it into a youtube video and share the powerpoint I used along with it. If I get asked the same question enough times I will turn it into a blog post or video. I also offer up 'intern' opportunities for folks who want to learn in person sales. And if you want something more in depth, check out my book "Create Your Way to Freedom! How

To Be A Big Success From Someone Who Isn't!" Check out **www.talesbybob.com/education**

Podcasts!

Bob does a lot podcasting. You should go to his website, **www.talesbybob.com** (noticing a theme here?), and check them out. Most of them are related to books in some way, but not all! His best known historically has been Books, Beards, Booze.

Book Clubs!

Want to read this book as part of your book club? Reach out! If you are close enough, I might come speak to it (especially if yall have good snacks). If you are farther away, I might be available to speak to your group remotely. At the bare minimum I will shoot you an email with some bonus content of some sort, and some book club discussion questions. Just us the contact form on my website, **www.talesbybob.com/contact**

About Bearded Bard Inkworks

A real human book publisher, who puts out novels and ttrpgs!

Here at Bearded Bard Inkworks, we are human people, who put out books, and things like books. Booky things. With actual pages. And ink. Except when they're digital of course. Either way, we're absolutely people, and not at all three octopuses pretending to be book publishers. Just look at the top hats. Only a human could be so fashionable.

Look, we love books here at Bearded Bard Inkworks. We do. But we also love rpgs. And general weirdness. So we seek out authors who are exploring unique spaces, while also generating cool tabletop games. Because who doesn't love the idea of finding that next book they love, and then getting to play a game in that world?

Learn more at **www.beardedbardinkworks.com**

Struggling with Drug Addiction?

If you or someone you know is struggling with drug addiction and want to get help, then call the number below. It is the Substance Abuse and Mental Health Services Administration help line, a confidential, free, 24-hour-a-day, 365-day-a-year, information service, in English and Spanish, for individuals and family members facing mental and/or substance use disorders. This service provides referrals to local treatment facilities, support groups, and community-based organizations. Callers can also order free publications and other information.

1-800-662-HELP (4357)

For more information you can visit their website here:

www.samhsa.gov/